Cinder's eyes sparkled with excitement. "I'll bet my residual check that Ferris will become a woman by the end of the summer."

Everyone stopped what they were doing, staring at each other. Then they turned expectantly towards Cinder.

"How much?" Angel said.

Cinder pointed to the check pinned to her wall above her photograph. "A hundred dollars, compliments of Tidy Curl."

Ferris' face was burning with embarrassment, confusion, but she realized that this was her chance to be accepted by these girls. "What do I have to do?" she asked.

"Just, uh, just let nature take its course," Cinder explained. "It's a contest. Ferris against . . ." She glanced at Angel. "No, you wouldn't have the guts."

Angel sucked her teeth and said, "You just lost a hundred bucks, creep."

Cinder shrieked with laughter. "Wow, this is going to be something else. Angel versus Ferris. Whoever loses her virginity first wins."

PARAMOUNT PICTURES PRESENTS

A STEVE FRIEDMAN/KINGS ROAD PRODUCTION

TATUM O'NEAL   KRISTY McNICHOL

LITTLE DARLINGS

ARMAND ASSANTE

PRODUCED BY STEPHEN J. FRIEDMAN

SCREENPLAY BY KIMI PECK AND DALENE YOUNG

STORY BY KIMI PECK

DIRECTED BY RONALD F. MAXWELL
A PARAMOUNT PICTURE

Little Darlings

A novel by Sonia Pilcer

**Based on the screenplay
by Kimi Peck and Dalene Young**

Story by Kimi Peck

BALLANTINE BOOKS • NEW YORK

Library of Congress Catalog Card Number: 80-80920

ISBN 0-345-28894-7

Manufactured in the United States of America

First Edition: April 1980

1

CARRYING a torn plaid suitcase held together by a plastic belt, Angel Bright walked away from the pre-fab flat they'd been living in for the past three years. They moved around a lot. That is, whenever her mother's newest boyfriend got tired and split the scene. This time, it was just the two of them scraping by, in the dregs of blue-collar paradise.

But Angel didn't care much. At fifteen, she wasn't into landscapes, sunsets, nature or anything like that. She puffed on her cigarette, clutched her transistor radio to her ear and kept walking, her dark hair swinging.

She passed a fenced yard where local boys played stick ball among shards of broken glass. But she didn't stop. A senile old man in a shabby coat hobbled by her, his cane nearly tripping her. She leaped off the curb, then leaped on. A middle-aged woman in a flowered smock sat singing to herself on the stoop, sipping a Yoo-Hoo.

A teenage boy in a torn t-shirt that said Starship in balloon letters shoved his third finger in front of her face. She tried to walk past him but he blocked her

1

way, starting to laugh like it was a real scream. Angel smiled slyly as she backed up, then kicked him between the legs. As he clutched himself, howling with pain, she asked, "How's it going, Charlie?" Then she took the cigarette out of her mouth and flicked it at him.

Suddenly, an arm grabbed her roughly.

"Hey, wait a second!" she said, turning to discover her mother who yanked her by the arm and dragged her to the beat-up old Chevy convertible parked nearby.

"What's wrong?" Angel demanded.

"You know I don't like you smoking," she said, opening the car door.

"Why the hell not?"

"Get in," her mother insisted.

"Damn it," she grumbled as she climbed into the car. Her mother slammed the door behind her.

She sat slumped in the car seat, watching her mother drive and attempt to retouch her makeup at the same time. As they just missed hitting a bus, Angel said, "You drive like shit." Then she paused, turning to her mother, "I don't want to go."

"You're going," she said, painting her mouth a screaming orange with a lipstick brush. She peered into the rear-view mirror.

"Says who?"

"Your social worker, that's who."

She slumped even lower into the seat, switching on the radio. As she turned from station to station, she glanced at her mother. She must have really been something once. If only she didn't put all that crap on her face and dress like Miss New Jersey, 1950 in tight, low-cut leotard tops and hip huggers. People said they looked alike.

Angel had short dark hair, a grown-out shag,

which she tended to brush back with her hand as if she couldn't be bothered with her appearance. But her body was tight and athletic, just about to sprout hips and a bust, very appealing.

She changed the station again, found bland country music, then stared anxiously outside the window. Her eyes were dark pits that revealed a great sadness and vulnerability not quite hidden by a tough glint.

"I didn't have time to label your underwear," her mother began. "I was going to—"

"Good," Angel said. "Nobody'll know who all the holes belong to."

"You better watch your mouth," she frowned, pursing her lips disapprovingly. Then she turned to look at her daughter. "Honey, I'm really gonna miss you. You know that?"

"So let me stay home. Please! I'll do anything," Angel pleaded. "They're going to treat me like the charity case. I know it. Here comes Angel, our token delinquent. Terrific."

"It's a scholarship," her mother insisted. "Why do you have to be so negative? You ought to be happy to—"

"Crap!" Angel exclaimed. "Nobody else there'll be on a scholarship."

"Angel! Listen, that's no way to begin—"

"How'd you like to spend your summer with a bunch of goody-goody creeps at sleepaway camp? It's going to be awful!" She turned the volume all the way up, saying softly, as if to herself, "Screw this." She stared down at her Woolworth sneakers, lousy jeans and the car's red upholstery or what was left of it.

"Did you ever go to camp?" Angel asked.

"Me?" Her mother turned to her, amused. "Are you kidding? I had to work every summer."

"What'd you do?"

She shook her head. "Waitress, what else?"

"At least you didn't have to go to camp," Angel said. "It's going to be awful."

They reached the highway. Her mother leaned out of the window. "Check if anything's coming from your direction."

Angel gave a whistle. "Look at that," she said, pointing to a black Rolls-Royce in the next lane.

As her mother entered the service road, she told Angel, "You know, I used to date this rich guy, Herb. He had a Mercedes, a boat, the works. But do you know what?"

"What?" Angel asked impatiently.

"I couldn't stand him and he had bad breath."

She laughed, muttering, "You're a real pisser, Mom."

Ferris Whitney sat glumly in the back of her father's black Rolls-Royce. He smiled at her in the rear-view mirror, saying approvingly, "Sharp outfit."

She stared down at her white silk suit. "They'll hate me. I just know it." Her sand-colored hair fell into her eyes.

He turned to her mother, an elegant woman with short frosted hair who was smoking a cigarette. "Did you pick it out for her?"

She nodded coolly. "It's a good color for Ferris."

"Are you sure?" she asked nervously. "I wanted to look casual, uh, not pretentious or like a snob— like the other girls . . ." She leaned over the seat to get her mother's attention.

"Don't do that, dear," her mother said, brushing her shoulder.

"I'm sorry."

Ferris leaned back, staring into the space between her parents through the windshield. She had an intense seriousness that made her seem older than fifteen. This was partly from having lived abroad and gone to schools where they spoke about good breeding and manners, where she felt like a Martian among Venusians.

Her blue eyes were engaging and when she smiled, they twinkled mischievously. Ferris had inherited her mother's English fair skin but not her mannequin-like body nor her poise.

She looked longingly at her mother. Ferris had worshipped her ever since she could remember, as did her father. Both were her admirers, her fan club, but sometimes it seemed as if neither one of them existed for her. She would busy herself with charity teas and fund-raising black tie dinners. That was when she seemed most content. Most of the time though, she was like a Snow Queen, beautiful and remote.

"You'll have a great time," her father said, turning momentarily to meet her eyes. "Don't worry, pumpkin."

"I'll die if he calls me that in front of anyone," she muttered. "You won't, will you?"

He smiled warmly. "I promise."

Her father couldn't be more different from her mother. Although an executive of a liquor corporation, he was like a big, huggable puppy dog sometimes. They roughhoused together on the back lawn, threw baskets and often had dinner for two in fancy restaurants when her mother was otherwise occupied.

There was a sadness about him that confused her, sometimes frightening her. Of late, he and her mother fought behind the closed door of their bedroom. Several times she had found her father sleeping in his study. There was a truce now, but she could feel the tension between them.

"Do we have to drive so fast?" she asked.

"We're late," her father said. "Where is that Sportsorama lot anyway?"

Ferris sank back into the soft leather of the seat. "I'm not going to fit in," she declared.

"Besides," he said, trying to make a joke, "I thought teeny-boppers liked speed."

"Daddy, I'm not a—" She looked at him, shaking her head with exasperation. Then she turned to her mother. "Do you really think I look okay?"

Her mother lit another cigarette with a thin gold lighter. "Like a million dollars."

"But that's just the way I don't want to look," she said softly. "So they'll all know. It always happens and then—"

The limousine pulled off the highway. "Which way do we go now?" he asked.

"Could you drop me off here?" Ferris asked.

"How many more years of adolescence?" he teased.

"Ferris hates the car," her mother observed.

"It's sort of gross," she tried to explain without hurting her father's feelings. "I mean, it's kind of, uh, embarrassing." She looked from her mother to him, watching his face change from a jaunty easiness to an expression of despondency. "I'm sorry, Dad. I really am . . ." She touched his arm.

"Does it say which way we should turn?" he asked, passing the Camp Little Wolf brochure to Ferris. "Would you please check it?"

"It doesn't say," Ferris declared. "Maybe we won't find it . . ."

"I have an instinct about it," he said. "It's right. I'm almost sure of that."

"Darling," her mother interrupted. "Shouldn't we ask—"

"It's this way," he insisted, turning right at the stop sign. Sportsorama was five hundred yards in the opposite direction.

2

ALTHOUGH the Sportsorama parking lot was full of cars, one couldn't miss the yellow school bus with CAMP LITTLE WOLF printed on both sides in black letters and about fifty squealing, verging on hysterical teenage and pre-teenage girls in varying stages of adolescent madness. Some sported Farrah Fawcett hairdos, others wore pigtails with matching bows. Every puckering stage of sexual development was in attendance and the girls checked each other out, forming mental pecking orders with furtive glances. Their parents stood nearby in mutual bewilderment.

Some unloaded trunks, complaining of bad backs, while a few clutched Kleenex in long-drawn-out tearful goodbyes. Promises to write, if not every day, every second day, were solicited by most. The girls giggled uncontrollably.

A Day-Glo-streaked van pulled up next to the bus. A bearded middle-aged hippy in a cowboy hat sat at its helm. His wife wore several strings of beads over a floral sack, and an Indian scarf tied around her head. As soon as the van came to a stop, a lovely young girl, about fourteen, leaped out. "We made it!" She did an expressive pirouette.

"Sunshine!" her mother called from the window. "Now we don't want you to get all hyped-up while you're away. Remember, go easy on the amino acids. And don't forget your mantra."

"I will," she said pleasantly, resembling an Herbal Essence madonna with tiny flowers in a wreath around her long golden hair. "Darn," she whispered, pushing a flower out of her face.

"Don't forget your vitamins," her father said, passing her an embroidered bag that was filled to the top. "They're all here." She dropped it over her shoulder.

He unlocked the back of the van and took out a khaki knapsack, a guitar case and a bag of food. "The bran's here," he said, "just in case. And there are some sprouts that should be ready soon. And some honey." He put his arms around his daughter. "It's the A and D which are really important. And the multiple, of course. You'll remember, won't you?"

"Don't worry, Dad," Sunshine said. "Really!"

"Who's worried?" he asked. "Worry is a totally unnecessary emotion. It doesn't do anything, like guilt. It's just that we want you to have a positive experience, to grow as a person . . ."

Her mother joined them, stroking Sunshine's hair. "Maybe when you get back, you can start est. We're going for some graduate seminars."

She wrinkled her nose. "I didn't like that lecture you took me to." Sunshine stared eagerly at a group of girls who were talking excitedly. "I better put my stuff on the bus," she said.

Her father grabbed the knapsack and guitar case while Sunshine gave her mother a warm hug. "A lot of good vibrations here," she said. "I can feel the energy. It's really heavy."

She picked up the food bag and ran to catch up with her father. "The enzyme digestants are real important," her mother called. "And don't eat sugar if you can help it . . ."

"I won't. Bye, Mom."

"Is that Dennis Hopper?" a girl asked as her father placed her knapsack and guitar case on the bus.

"I bet it's him," another one whispered. "He looks exactly like him in *Easy Rider*."

Sunshine smiled. "Did you hear that, Dad?"

He shrugged his shoulders. "A lot of people around here are into physical reality," he muttered.

"Yeah."

A maroon station wagon overpacked with freckled, chestnut-haired children came to a raucous halt. "We're here, Carrots!" a ten-year-old boy screamed. "Look at all those cars."

"Let me out of here!" his sister shouted from under a pile of her brothers who attempted to play touch football in the back of the car. "Come on, you guys!"

A pert face covered with a galaxy of freckles followed by a neck and finally a body in a pair of overalls forced its way out of the huddle. Her glorious red hair, gathered in pigtails, reached her waist.

"I can hardly believe it!" she cried with joy as she jumped to the ground. "Six whole weeks of peace."

"Have a good time, Cathy," her mother, similarly freckled, called from the front seat. "But don't get in any trouble this time." She turned around. "Quiet back there! Stop fighting!"

Her father, who wore a golfing hat, added, "You heard your mother. Be a good girl."

"Ha ha!" She wiggled her hands on her ears, making a face for the benefit of all four of her younger brothers. "You can't come! Because you're all babies—and dumb too!" She ran to the bus with her father following behind in the car.

Dana Wells arrived in a taxi, still reading her book after the cab had stopped. "Oh, one minute," she said, adjusting her wire-frame glasses as she squinted to read the fare. She searched in her bag for her wallet. "I know I've got it," she said, emptying her jean pockets. "Oh, yeah. Here it is."

She paid the driver, who helped her with her suitcase. "Thank you, sir."

"Jesus, this weighs a ton," he remarked. "What are you smuggling, cinder blocks?"

She eyed him with a sophisticated toss of her head. "I happen to read a lot." She paused pregnantly, then added, "I love ideas." Her eyebrows wriggled above her glasses.

As she walked toward the bus, she picked up her paperback book and began reading again. Her suitcase dragged on the ground.

Dana's clothes fitted her as if she got dressed in the dark; her jeans bagged in all the wrong places, yet they pulled across her rather generous seat. Long brown hair was clipped in a schoolmarmish ponytail and long silver earrings dangled from her ears. She inhabited her body the way someone entered a museum—quietly.

A Land Rover with the top down parked several feet from the bus. The couple began making out on the front seat.

"Oh, baby, I'm going to miss you so much," her boyfriend whispered, kissing her neck. "I wish we could stay together."

"Me too," Cinder muttered as she looked around the parking lot. "This is going to be a major bore. Camp," she said contemptuously. "What a drag." She pouted her thickly glossed mouth.

Cinder wore dark glasses which made her look like a Hollywood-bound starlet. Her boyfriend, Robbie, looked helplessly in love with her. She shared his sentiment.

She ran her fingers through her thick mane of stylishly permed hair. "I guess I might as well get this over with." She kissed him provocatively on the mouth, her tongue teasing his. When he grabbed her, she said, "Gotta go."

As she walked toward the bus, her feet quivered slightly from the height of her heels. But wasn't that the price one paid for beauty, and hence power?

A long line of girls toting suitcases and duffel bags waited to have their names checked off on a list.

"What's taking so long?" complained a chubby youngster in a Patti Smith t-shirt. "I can't believe this."

"Hey, pipsqueak!" an older girl from the front of the line called. "Pipe down."

"The name's Penelope," she said with some arrogance. "For your information."

A handsome dark-haired young man with a clipboard in his hands studied the girls, his expression alternating between sternness and boyish grinning. "There are still some girls missing." He glanced at his list.

"Women," eleven-year-old Penelope corrected him.

"Right." Gary Callahan checked his watch. Fifteen more minutes. So many adolescent girls clamoring around him, bursting out of their tank tops and patched pants, unnerved him.

"Have a groovy time and all," Sunshine's father called from the van as he started the motor.

"Peace, baby. We'll see you on Parents' Day," her mother said, waving her fingers in a peace sign as they drove away.

She smiled and nodded unsurely, looking around herself before she returned a hasty peace sign, then entered the bus. She hoped no one had seen them.

Dana continued reading as she dragged her suitcase across the parking lot and bumped into Cinder, who was waving to her boyfriend.

"Hey, watch it!" Dana cried after it was too late. "Oh, no!"

Her suitcase popped open and a dozen books tumbled out.

"What are you, a librarian?" Cinder asked, helping her pick up the books. Dana still read her book.

"Get this," she exclaimed. "According to the Aztec legend, the high priests would blow cocaine into the vagina of the virgin bride with a fertility pipe to anesthetize her hymen!" She bit her fingernail, chewing on it.

"I'll remember that on my wedding night," Cinder remarked sarcastically. "What is all this?" She began to read some of the titles aloud. *"The Joy of Sex, My Secret Garden, Erotic Fantasies of Men, Selected Poems of Robert Browning—"*

"Hi, I'm Dana Wells," she said. "My friends call me the porno scholar."

"Cindy Spillman, but my boyfriend calls me Cinder because he says I'm so hot." She licked her lips.

"Was that him in the Land Rover?"

Cinder nodded proudly. "Isn't he something?"

"Hot, hot, hot," Dana said.

Both grinned as if they shared a secret, boarding the bus together.

"You don't know how hot."

At the sight of Cinder in her tight pants and high heels, Gary raised his eyebrows.

Sportsorama was down the next block. The Chevy ran a red light.

"Let me off here, will you?" Angel said, her eyes dark and forlorn, biting her lip. "I can walk from here."

"What's the matter?" her mother asked. "You ashamed of me?"

"It's not you," she answered, looking out the window. "This car sucks." Her voice was unsteady.

"Angel—" Her mother tried to put her arm around her but she shook it off.

"Cut it out! Come on, Mom!"

"It won't be so bad," her mother said. "Maybe you'll even make a friend or two, huh?"

Angel laughed bitterly. "That'll be the day."

"It could happen, you know. If you don't go there with a chip on your shoulder."

As her mother drove through a stop sign, turning sharply to miss the psychedelic van, Angel said, "You really think you'll be okay?"

"I'm a big girl," her mother teased.

As they turned into the driveway of the parking lot, the Chevy's muffler gave way to old age and fell, dragging along the pavement in a shower of sparks. Several of the girls and their parents turned to look disdainfully at the noisy car.

"What are they getting so uptight about?" her mother said.

Angel stared back at them, her anger rising. As she was about to storm out of the car, her mother grabbed her arm. "Angel, sweetie," she began, her voice straining for control, "I know it's difficult, your first time going away . . ."

Angel avoided meeting her mother's eyes, afraid that she had become sentimental and mushy.

"Six weeks isn't that long . . ." She brushed Angel's hair out of her eyes. "Honey—"

Embarrassed, Angel turned away. "G'bye, Mom," she said softly. "I know I'm going to hate it."

"Be good," her mother said as Angel began walking toward the bus, her suitcase knocking against her side. "Or I'll break your little buns when I see you!"

"You too!" Angel called, turning back to look at her.

Her mother smiled sadly and pulled out of the parking lot, with the clatter of her muffler dragging along the ground. She wondered what she would do without her daughter who had been her buddy, confidante, roommate. It's good for the kid, she told herself, to be with other girls her own age. But she was going to miss Angel more than she could bear to think about.

3

As Angel entered the bus, the girls' stares buzzed around her like a swarm of bees. She took a deep breath and slowly walked down the aisle, taking a seat in the back by herself.

Gary checked his watch again. He called the girls' names. "Carter? Walker? Wells? Spillman? Bright? Oh, you're here. Good. Whitney? Where's Whitney?" They looked blankly at him.

As soon as he finished, the girls began talking at once, interrupting each other, laughing loudly, their voices high-pitched, bouncing on their seats with excited anticipation. Angel sat on her hands, staring impassively ahead of herself.

"I saw *Grease* six times," Carrots said proudly. "I love Olivia Newton-John."

"Did anyone see Cocteau's *Beauty and the Beast?*" Sunshine asked. "It's so beautiful . . ." She sighed. "And romantic . . ."

"My fiancé looks exactly like John Travolta," Cinder said.

"Honest?" Carrots asked, her eyes wide with wonder.

"I saw *Last Tango in Paris* ten times," Dana said. "Do you remember the margarine scene? Can you imagine someone doing that? Wow!" She stood up and bent over.

"You know who I just love," Carrots confided. "Andy Gibb." She wrapped her arms around herself.

"I love his ass," Chubby said. "It's so small. Tweak!" She grabbed the air.

Glaring out the window, Angel took a cigarette out of her pocket. Cinder spotted her and whispered to Dana, "Get her."

Angel heard it, hesitated momentarily, then put the cigarette in her mouth. Damn all of them. Chicks were so catty.

"Smoking impairs a man's ability to sustain sexually," Dana remarked knowledgeably.

Angel struck the match defiantly and lit her cigarette.

"So does alcohol," Dana added.

"Are you really engaged?" Carrots turned to Cinder, awed out of her gourd. "Like it's official or something."

She nodded. "My parents think sending me to camp will cool it off with Robbie. No way." She shrugged. "They're so provincial."

"Yeah," Carrots said, continuing to stare at Cinder. "Mine too. They treat me like a baby." She wriggled her nose so that all the freckles there danced.

"Sensuality is an important part of life," Sunshine announced.

Angel took a deep drag of her cigarette. As she released the smoke in perfect rings, she muttered to herself, "Jerks." But her expression was full of longing.

As the motor revved up and the parents screamed their last, anxious goodbyes, "Remember, we love you . . . Behave yourself . . . Don't get into trouble . . . If you need anything, phone us . . . Don't forget to write to your aunt . . . Eat everything they give you . . . ," the girls peered out of the windows. They waved frantically, some standing on their seats, others on tiptoes, blowing kisses, cursing under their breath, "Shit, are they going to stand around all day?" Finally, the bus started to move. "Hooray!" Carrots shouted.

About to leave the parking lot, they heard a screeching sound. When the black Rolls-Royce braked loudly, stopping in front of the bus and blocking its way, Cinder whistled. "What have we here?"

Ferris leaped out of the car, carrying her designer suitcase, matching shoulder satchel and her sleeping bag. "Stop!" she screamed. "Hey, you! Busdriver! Stop!"

The bus halted and a moment later, the door opened. Gary checked the list. "Ferris Whitney?" he asked.

"Yes," she said breathlessly, staring at him. "I'm sorry but we got lost."

He smiled, motioning for her to climb in. "Okay, everyone's here," he said. "Let's get this madhouse on the road."

He shut the door behind her. She darted around to see her father backing the Rolls up. He stopped to wave to her. She waved back to him. Her mother looked absently out the window.

Ferris wanted to call to her but knew it was useless. At least she came to see her off. Finally she turned to face the girls. She smiled uncomfortably, realizing they had watched the whole scene, Rolls and all. Move it, one foot in front of the other, she commanded herself.

As she walked down the aisle of the bus, Ferris felt extremely self-conscious. Everyone wore jeans except for her. She wished she could flee: out of the bus, away from her parents, somewhere. But she was here and stuck. She stopped, searching for an empty seat. They were all occupied except for the one next to Angel. She made her way to the back, passing Cinder, who leaned into the aisle.

"Well, well . . ." Cinder checked out her outfit, from the collar of her shirt to the cuff of her pants. Ferris extended her hand awkwardly.

"Hi," she said.

"So tacky," Cinder declared loudly. Ferris withdrew her hand. "And ostentatious . . ."

"What's that?" Carrots asked. "Osten—"

"Later," Dana said, studying the two girls.

Angel observed them too. The rich girl in her fancy clothes. And the other one, a bitch if she ever saw one. Angel hated privilege, bucks to burn, people having everything they wanted just because of who they happened to be born. It was unfair. Yet, this girl didn't seem snobbish or conceited. In fact, she looked as scared as anybody. But Angel was not about to give her the benefit of the doubt. No way. Besides, watching how the other girls reacted to her gave her the idea that this might be her in, an opportunity to carve her own place in the group.

As Ferris approached, Angel sprawled out, placing her legs across the empty seat. She looked around to see if anyone noticed. A couple of girls had and giggled nervously. Angel announced, showing off, "Looks like cod liver oil. Hard to swallow."

Everyone laughed at that. She was pleased. Maybe they'd like her after all. If she played her cards right.

Ferris, still unaware that it was she who was being laughed at, smiled as she stopped in front of Angel's seat. She began tentatively, "My name is—"

"This seat's taken," Angel interrupted.

Ferris recognized her adversary immediately. "By who?" she demanded, refusing to relent.

"My guardian angel." Angel smirked at the cleverness of her own remark. Around them, the girls stirred, whispering and laughing with breathless excitement.

For a moment, Ferris studied them, catching on to the joke—namely, herself. What a scream. She pushed Angel's legs aside and sat down on the seat.

"She'll have to sit on my lap," Ferris retorted.

The laughter grew louder. Angel knew it was her move. She was determined not to lose them. She thought fast.

"She's a he," Angel returned.

"Then I'll just have to sit on his lap," Ferris answered.

There was more laughter as the girls crowded around them. "Beat it," Angel said menacingly. "Do you hear me?"

"Make me." Ferris sat squarely in her seat, waiting to see what her opponent would do.

At that, Angel shoved her, trying to force Ferris out of the seat. But she refused to budge, crossing her arms stubbornly. Angel pushed harder then, standing over her. The other girls hung over their seats, applauding, cheering them on. "A fight!" some screamed. "There's going to be a fight!"

When Angel took a slug at her jaw, Ferris returned a blow of equal impact. Angel bounced back on her seat, stunned. Soon they were all over each other, pulling hair, biting, trying their hardest to wipe the other one out.

All the girls cheered, choosing their favorite, except for a concerned Sunshine who sighed. "People who eat meat are so aggressive. It's all that blood."

No one paid any attention to her. "Get her!" they screamed. "You're not going to take that, are you!"

"Wow!" Carrots said, dazed. "Look at them go! This never happened last year."

Dana punched Penelope on the arm lightly. "What a right that girl's got!"

"Watch it," Penelope said, brushing her off.

Just then, the bus pulled over to the side of the road, and came to a screeching stop. Gary ran to the back. He had to force his way through the girls, who were oblivious to everything but the fight. "Clear out!" he called. "Coming through."

The girls turned expectantly toward him. He studied them, one by one. They had the same expressions as boxing fans.

"What's the problem?" he asked angrily.

When he got to the center of the storm, he found Ferris and Angel sitting next to each other, staring in opposite directions.

"Well?" he asked.

"No problem," Angel said, keeping her hands in the pockets of her jeans.

Ferris' white silk suit was covered with dark sneaker footprints. She looked down at herself and gestured with her hands as if she hadn't the slightest idea as to their source. Secretly, she was pleased.

Gary scowled and made his way forward to his seat. With a jerk which startled them all, the bus started moving again.

4

MAINLY, it was miles of highway. And some flat farmland. But the girls were too busy psyching each other out to notice. An hour and a half had passed.

"Rest stop!" Gary announced, opening the bus door. "Everybody do what they have to do," he shouted as the girls charged out of the door.

Ferris stopped to glance at the counselor. His dark, moody good looks attracted her. She smiled at him, pushing a sandy strand of hair out of her face.

"Fifteen minutes!" he shouted. "You better all be back by then." He grinned at Ferris. "We got to have some discipline around here. You okay?" She nodded.

Rest stop, U.S.A. How come they all looked exactly alike, Angel mused as she waited in line outside the ladies room. There was a small patch of grass, with two picnic tables and a couple of vending machines. Miss Rolls-Royce joined her on line. Ferris, like the wheel. She turned her off.

"Hey!" Carrots exclaimed. "Where'd you guys learn to fight like that?"

"Madison Square Garden," Angel muttered.

23

"I'm Cathy Carter." She introduced herself, eyes shining with friendly good-naturedness. Maybe it was the red hair and freckles that did that, Angel thought as she looked at her.

"Everyone calls her Carrots," Sunshine added, joining their small circle. "I'm Sunshine."

Angel nodded. "Angel Bright."

"Sounds like something at the top of a Christmas tree," Ferris snickered.

"Oh, yeah?" Angel grabbed her roughly.

"Wait, you guys!" Sunshine interrupted anxiously. "I've got some vitamin E and niacin."

They stopped for a moment, staring at their fragile-looking mediator. "Niacin," she assured them. "It keeps you from freaking out."

Sunshine reached into her bag and pulled out a bottle of niacin. Angel shook her head in disbelief, declining the white pills. Ferris took one pill graciously.

"I'm Ferris Whitney," she said to Carrots and Sunshine. Her back was turned to Angel.

Inside the bathroom Cinder combed her thick hair. As she stared into the mirror, her expression was of pure, consummate love. Dana sat perched on the large wastepaper basket, reading her book, while Penelope furtively stuffed toilet paper down the neck of her t-shirt into her bra.

"Oh, God," she wailed. "They'll never grow."

"No wonder," Cinder said, staring at her in the mirror. "You're smothering them." Then she stuck out her chest and smiled seductively at her own reflection. When Angel offered cigarettes around, ignoring Ferris, Cinder took one. She held it, unlit, posing with it in her right hand.

"Great hair," Angel said sarcastically.

"Thanks." Cinder smiled, unaware of the sarcasm.

"Oh, God!" Dana exclaimed, looking up from her book momentarily. "Can you imagine doing it with a German shepherd?"

"Yuck!" Carrots gasped. "How gross."

"You look familiar," Ferris said, looking shrewdly at Cinder.

"You've probably seen me on TV," she answered haughtily.

Angel turned to her, hostility in her voice. "In what? A Brillo commercial?"

"I'm the 'before girl' in the Tidy Tangles creme rinse commercial," she declared, lifting her hair with her hands and then dropping it dramatically so it billowed around her shoulders.

Angel interrupted her. "I'm out of matches. Anybody got a match?"

Cinder sent her an annoyed glance, then turned to the pleasure of her own reflection, continuing to try different poses with the cigarette.

From one of the toilet stalls, Sunshine called out, "Smoking causes lung cancer, emphysema, upper respiratory problems and it turns your teeth yellow . . ."

"Terrific!" Angel called. "A light, anyone?"

Penelope dug into the pockets of her jeans and handed a book of matches to Angel. She stared curiously at Penelope, who came up to her shoulder. "I don't believe it."

She shrugged. "I eat them. Just the tips, not the stems or anything." She glanced around defensively. "They taste good."

As Sunshine exited from the toilet, she added, "And the paper is high in fiber content. It's not very healthy."

Angel lit her cigarette. As she was about to offer

a light to Cinder, she realized that she had no need
for it. So she tossed the book of matches back to
Penelope saying, "Get your butt out of here, squirt."

"Pushy mothers," Penelope grumbled, stuffing another wad of paper into her pathetic bosom.

As Penelope walked out of the bathroom, she
cursed the fate of being only ten years old, which
meant that everyone treated her like a kid. But she
had thoughts, ideas, desires—all trapped inside of
her flat-chested body. One of these days, they'd feel
sorry.

Gary glanced at her, then knocked loudly on the
door. "Five more minutes, that's all!"

As he noticed Penelope's lumpy, lopsided breasts,
he almost exploded into a fit of laughter. But instead,
he restrained himself and messed her hair up playfully. "How you doing?"

"Everyone's so damn patronizing," she muttered
as she stomped off by herself, her back straight, her
face proudly posed toward the sky.

The talk was steaming up the mirrors inside the
bathrom. Angel casually blew smoke into Ferris'
face, making her cough. She sent Angel a pissed
look, but it was Dana who engaged her attention.

"I knew a girl who did it on a roller coaster,"
Dana announced proudly. "She said it was the best
experience of her life. Ecstasy! Multiple orgasm!"
she cried.

Ferris turned away disapprovingly and began to
wash her face. But the other girls cried excitedly,
"Really? They did it there? Wasn't it dangerous?"

Dana grinned, pleased by the attention. "Where's
the weirdest place you've ever done it?" she asked,
turning to Ferris.

She was wiping her face with a paper towel. "None

of your business," she said, trying to cut off the subject.

Cinder joined her. "Why not?" she demanded of Ferris. Then she turned to the other girls. "She probably doesn't know anything."

"I know enough," Ferris said quietly.

"Been to fourth base?" Cinder asked.

"All the way?" Dana added definitively.

"I'm fifteen!" Ferris cried. "Nobody goes to fourth base until—"

"I hit a home run at fourteen," Cinder said triumphantly.

Ferris was caught offguard, suddenly unsure of herself. She turned to Sunshine and Carrots. "Have you?"

They looked at each other, then nodded haltingly.

"What about you?" Ferris confronted Dana.

"Of course," she said, her face becoming red. "Sure, uh, you don't think I spend all my time reading, do you?"

A silence followed as each of the girls avoided facing one another, afraid that they would be found out. Finally Cinder declared loudly, "Well, it looks like some of us are women . . ." She smiled self-contentedly. "And . . . some are, I guess, little girls . . ."

Then she turned to Angel. "What are you?"

Angel gazed at her, unwilling to lie. "Boys are a pain in the ass," she said.

Cinder laughed. "Two little virgins . . . how quaint. No wonder you two are always fighting." She studied Ferris, then Angel. "All that unreleased energy. It can really upset a girl . . ."

Angel glared at Cinder, who continued, looking for support from the others. "They're probably lezes," she sneered.

Everyone began to laugh. Carrots and Sunshine giggled uncomfortably. Dana howled, slapping her knee. The tension in the room made them all feel slightly unhinged, giddy. Angel and Ferris stood there, helpless and angry.

Ferris cut into the laughter. "Maybe she is," she stared at Angel. "But I'm straight."

"Prove it," Cinder said.

"How?" she asked.

Cinder licked her lips, biding her time. She looked at the other girls, who now appeared nervous, shifting their weight from foot to foot. Carrots swallowed loudly. "My gum," she whispered.

"Lose your cherry, stupid," she said.

"What?" Ferris asked.

"Don't you even know what that is?" Cinder sneered.

"Well, sure . . ."

"So?"

A sense of fright clutched at Ferris' throat, but she nodded. "Why not?" she said, trying to regain her composure.

Cinder turned to face Angel. "What about you, smut mouth?"

"What about me?" Angel glared angrily at her.

"I think you're into girls."

"Oh, yeah?" Angel lunged furiously at her. Cinder darted to the other side of the room, laughing. "Did you see that? She tried to grab my tit!"

"EVERYBODY OUT!" Gary screamed, pushing the door open. "The bus is leaving right now."

5

CHUGGING and creaking along an unpaved road, the springs of its seats groaning, the bus finally pulled up to the grounds of Camp Little Wolf. Angel winced as she eyed the girls in white camp shorts and t-shirts, several jogging, others carrying tennis and badminton rackets. There was grass everywhere. Trees too.

How was she ever going to *take* all this fresh air and wholesomeness? It was unbearable. Angel lit a cigarette.

The counselors waited by the bus. Angel was the first to get off. Before she knew it, someone had taken her smoke. As she was about to protest, she noticed an attractive young woman smiling at her. Angel grinned sheepishly at her.

Cinder, Dana, Sunshine, Carrots and some of the other girls walked out of the bus, chattering excitedly. They headed directly for their cabin, familiar with the grounds. They whooped happily as they repeated stories from previous years. Ferris followed a few feet behind them, not sure if she should walk with them.

Cinder whispered conspiratorially to the girls, who giggled and turned to look at Ferris. She ignored them, although she knew that she was the subject of their riotous laughter. As Ferris noted the rows of identical white cabins and the enormous dining hall, she wondered how she would last in Camp Little Wolf.

"Ferris probably isn't gay," Cinder said loudly. "Just sexually immature. I bet she'd go all the way if she had a chance."

Ferris blanched visibly but was determined not to reveal her own insecurity. Besides, she realized that her acceptance by these girls was on the line. So she said resolutely, "Sure, I'm ready."

Cinder grinned. "We'll see about that." She led the way on a stone-lined path. "Oh, hi, Chubby."

An overweight young girl trundled by.

Standing outside of cabin A, Diane, the counselor, called out names from the roll sheet. Only a few years older than her campers, she could recall her own fears on the first day of camp.

"Whitney, Sorrell, Hamilton . . ." She smiled at the girls.

When little Penelope, her bra stuffed to the hilt, tried to dart past her, Diane stopped her. "Hold it a moment," she said, amused. "Where do you think you're going?"

"You talking to me?" Penelope asked, all innocence.

"Name?"

"Penny—uh, Shubert . . . I'm kind of in a hurry . . ." She tried to walk past Diane again.

"You're in"—Diane said, looking at her list—"cabin C."

"Cabin C's for kids!" Penelope hooted, her face

becoming red and angry. "It's not fair. Not one bit. To be judged by your age . . ."

"I can't do—" She raised her eyebrows sympathetically.

"Oh, you don't know what it's like to be surrounded by ten-year-olds!" she wailed. "I'll go nuts! My brain's going to disintegrate." She slammed the screen door.

As she walked toward cabin C, she grumbled to herself. "That's what I call discrimination."

Inside cabin A, in one large room with wooden beams and tiny cubbyholes, the girls were busily unpacking, changing clothes, and hanging knick-knacks on the wall. A transistor radio blared loudly as Diane assigned bunks.

"Cathy Ann Carter and Dana Wells . . ." she announced. "The back bunk."

"Great!" Carrots exclaimed, smiling at Dana.

"You can read some of my books," Dana promised. *"The Story of O."*

"Oh, I don't know if I'd like that." Then she reconsidered, realizing that she didn't want her own inexperience to be found out, and said, "That's a good idea."

Cinder began decorating her own area immediately. She pinned up an eight by ten photograph of herself and then her residual check above that. She stood away from the wall, contemplating them.

Diane continued to assign bunks. "Ferris Whitney," she called. "And Angel Bright, over here."

"No way," Angel said stubbornly.

Ferris glared at her.

"C'mon, girls. These bunks have been assigned for months." She looked from Angel to Ferris, then back to Angel.

Ferris finally walked to the bunk. Diane turned to

Angel. "Oh, okay," Angel muttered as she walked over to the bunk.

They stared angrily at each other for several moments. Then Ferris brought her two suitcases to the bed. Angel tossed her duffel bag up on the upper bunk.

"I'm on top," Angel said.

"Big deal," Ferris answered coldly.

Angel climbed up to sit on the upper bunk, dangling her legs over the side, into Ferris' face. Then she began unpacking a six-pack of beer and several cartons of cigarettes.

"Look," Ferris said angrily. "I don't like sharing the bunk with you either. You keep out of my way and I'll keep out of yours. Deal?"

Angel shrugged, bringing her legs up on her bed. She lay down, using her duffel bag as a pillow, lighting up a cigarette. Ferris unpacked furtively, hiding some expensive clothes while she took out her most prized possession—a pair of worn jeans with holes on the knees. She laid them out on her bed.

"Get this," Dana called, reading out loud from *Looking for Mr. Goodbar*. " 'When she closed her eyes she saw Marvella's face next to Brooks' penis which jolted her more fully awake.' "

"I should hope so," Cinder said smartly.

"Yuk," Carrots booed. When Cinder's dark eyes turned to scrutinize her, she explained, "Uh, I don't go in for group sex, you know what I mean?"

Several minutes later, the door squeaked open. Everyone became silent. It was Penelope—carrying her sleeping bag. Carrots and Dana cried simultaneously, "Oh no!"

"You know what they're doing over there?" Penelope demanded. "Telling fairy stories! Can you believe it?"

"Fairy stories, huh?" Dana smirked.

Cinder touched Ferris' chiffon nightgown admiringly as she unpacked. "So *you,* my dear," she said sarcastically. "Pure, 99.9 percent pure."

Ferris was embarrassed. "My mom got it for me."

Upstairs Angel fiddled with her duffel bag which hardly had any clothes in it. She pulled out an extra t-shirt.

Cinder called to her cruelly, "What happened? Forget your wardrobe?"

Angel ignored her, so Cinder turned to the other girls. "God, I'm not used to sleeping solo. I don't even know if I'll be able to fall asleep." She stretched her arms languidly.

"Me either," Carrots agreed. "I bet I'll get insomnia."

"I think they put saltpeter in our hamburger. Like in the Army," Dana added knowledgeably.

"You shouldn't eat meat anyway," Sunshine pronounced. "It's full of male hormones."

"Ugh."

"I knew a girl who grew a moustache. It was horrible and she had to get depilated—all because she ate a bologna sandwich."

Cinder approached Ferris, her voice dropping gently. "Girls, we really have to help Ferris with her problem." She glanced up to Angel. "You're a lost cause," she sneered.

"Go to hell," Angel said.

She put her arm protectively around Ferris. "It's not hopeless, you know," she consoled. "It's time our Ferris experienced 'la dolce vita' . . ."

"What?" Angel asked.

"Technically speaking," Ferris translated, "it means the good life. You know, Fellini."

Cinder's eyes sparkled with excitement. "I'll bet my residual check—"

"Her what?" Sunshine asked, wriggling her nose with confusion.

"—that Ferris will become a woman by the end of summer."

Everyone stopped what they were doing, staring at each other. Then they turned expectantly toward Cinder.

"How much?" Angel asked.

Cinder pointed to the check pinned to her wall above her photograph. "A hundred dollars, compliments of Tidy Curl."

"Whoa!" Carrots yelled.

"That's a lot of moolah," Dana said.

Ferris' face was burning with embarrassment and confusion, but she realized that this was her chance. "What do I have to do?" she asked.

Dana snickered. "You make it sound like a job."

"Just, uh," Cinder pronounced, "let nature take its course."

"I don't get it," Sunshine said.

"It's a contest," Cinder explained condescendingly. "Ferris against . . ." She glanced at Angel. "No, you wouldn't have the guts."

Angel sucked her teeth and said, "You just lost a hundred bucks, creep."

Cinder shrieked with laughter. "Wow, this is going to be something else. Angel versus Ferris. Whoever loses her virginity first wins."

"I'll put ten dollars on her!" Dana said, pointing to Angel.

"Me too! She's got a mean right!"

"Count me in too!"

The girls screamed excitedly, placing bets. Ferris

sat on her bed, her legs weak, feeling frightened. Angel, above her, also sat quietly. Both of them were almost forgotten as Cinder collected the money. "Okay, I'll get some change for you . . ."

"How much would a Donny Osmond autograph be worth?"

"Two cents!"

"Five dollars on the girl in the white nightgown!"

"I'm on her team too!"

"Let's tell the other bunks too!"

"Yeah! We can get them into it—"

"Wouldn't that be great! Maybe they'll even put some money down."

"Sure," Angel muttered, lighting another cigarette, as she disappeared into her bunk. The smoke curled in ringlets, stealing out through the screen. She watched them, thinking how great it would be to fly like the light bugs that flickered outside.

No one noticed when Ferris left the room. Slowly she walked outside, the cool night air blowing her thin nightgown, sending goose bumps over her body. But she didn't care. It felt less oppressive than being inside with them. And yet she didn't want to be by herself. She wrapped her arms around herself.

For a moment, she stared into the window of the cabin. The light inside was yellow and warm. She could see all the girls but Angel clustered animatedly around Cinder.

"I'm on Ferris' team!" one called.

"Not me, Angel's tough."

"Yeah, but she seems more experienced. You know, mature."

"There's no doubt about it. The rich girl's got it made," Cinder declared confidently. "She'll win."

"My name's Ferris," she said quietly, looking up at the star-filled sky. One of these days she'd be her own person and it would not matter who her family was or what car her father drove. Until then, she had to deal with this crap.

6

THE first thing next morning, everyone was rallied around the flagpole, pledging allegiance. Angel blew on her right hand to keep warm, while she kept her other hand in the pocket of her jeans. The pulley on the rope squeaked loudly as the flag was hoisted to the top of the pole.

Afterwards, at assembly, Miss Nickels, a bird-like woman with a whistle around her neck, addressed the young ladies of Camp Little Wolf. Cinder, Ferris, Dana, Sunshine, Carrots and Angel sat in metal chairs in the front row of the social hall.

"And this is your music and art appreciation counselor, Diane Vogel, who I'm sure will give you hours of aesthetic experience . . ." Her voice was as shrill as chalk on a blackboard.

With her shiny brown hair and svelte figure, Diane looked radiant. She bowed slightly and polite applause followed. Her embarrassed smile revealed her own discomfort.

"Gary Callahan," Miss Nickels continued, nodding in his direction, "heads our physical well-being program."

At the sight of his dark hair and muscular body, several girls whistled. He smiled modestly.

"Ladies . . ." Miss Nickels cautioned, scrutinizing them with raised eyebrows. Then she shrugged her shoulders. "And you'll get to know Mary Kellerman, our wilderness training leader. She'll take you on some nature expeditions that—uh, will awaken all your five senses which can become so deadened—"

A chorus of moans followed.

Miss Nickels ignored them. "And, ladies, last but not least, Mr. Lido, who will educate you on the art of gardening, astronomy and bird watching."

A middle-aged man with a pair of binoculars around his neck waved to the girls, who applauded him until Miss Nickels called attention. He sat down contentedly, his bald pate gleaming.

"Crud," Carrots whispered to Cinder. "It's like school."

"At Little Wolf," Miss Nickels began once again, this time her hands held out to the girls, "we address ourselves to the whole woman. Girls, you're entering a new era . . ." She smiled with encouragement. "Puberty is waning. You're about to—"

Sunshine made a loud munching sound as she chewed on sunflower seeds. "Want some?"

"Shhh," someone called behind her.

"What's she talking about?" she asked Angel.

"Beats me," Angel said, frowning.

Miss Nickels continued. "This could be a primary kind of passage for you. I want to help prepare you for adulthood . . ."

"Talks like a damned dictionary," Angel sneered, upset that she didn't understand Miss Nickels' vocabulary.

"She happens to be well-read," Cinder remarked loftily. "Some of us are and some of us aren't. Right,

Ferris?" She leaned over to Ferris, who nodded with little enthusiasm.

"This summer, set a goal for yourself," Miss Nickels suggested, her eyes bright with inspiration. "Do something special, something you've never done before!"

Suddenly, the front row burst into giggles as the girls lightly elbowed Ferris and Angel.

"Hey, you guys," Angel whispered. "Quit it."

Diane looked quizzically in their direction. Cinder and Carrots put their hands over their mouths to keep from giggling.

"Too many of us aren't motivated to complete what we've begun," Miss Nickels continued, unaware of the interruption. "In every one of you, there's a special talent. And no two talents are alike. Let's find out what it is this summer and nurture it so it'll grow—" She made a bridge out of her hands.

"I hope no one gets knocked up!" Dana whispered.

"Choose a goal. Go after it with a positive attitude and, by golly, you might just achieve it. You'll never know if you don't try, right? Onward and upward, ladies!"

As soon as she finished, Carrots ran from the area, shrieking with laughter.

"Come on, Ferris!" Sunshine called from first base, waving her hand.

In the center of the baseball diamond, Angel was pitching. She had already tagged two girls out, and Ferris was up.

Angel took a step backwards, then threw the ball, missing Ferris' shoulder by two inches.

"Watch it!" Ferris called.

Angel sent her a pitch designed to blow Ferris'

head off of her shoulders. "There. Is that any better?" she muttered.

Ferris hit the wild pitch, running to first base and then to second, where Angel tagged her out. Meanwhile, Sunshine came home.

The mountain slanted at a ninety-degree incline. Nature hike. It was two hours. Diane led up front. "Come on, girls. We're almost to the top! You can make it."

Everyone looked grimy and exhausted except for Cinder, who wore fashionable terrycloth short-shorts and wedged espadrilles. "Are you having a hard time?" she asked the winded Dana.

"I've got my period," she moaned. "I swear I do. Why won't anyone believe me?"

As Cinder passed her, Dana continued miserably, ranting at the rocks and trees, "I'm just not into sports. I'm an intellectual. Five more weeks. Camp life is killing me."

Angel, one socked toe poking through her sneaker, walked at the head of the line with Diane. The sun had baked her face a rosy brown. She could hardly believe it. She was actually enjoying herself.

"Do you go climbing a lot?" Diane asked, impressed by Angel's athletic energy.

"Sure," she said. "Rooftops, fire escapes. Stuff like that. You've got to be able to climb in the city. You a mountain climber?"

"I have—"

Cinder strolled by them. "Darling shoes," she remarked, staring down at Angel's sneakers.

She ignored her but her expression turned grim, her dark eyes flashing. Angel dug into her pockets for a cigarette.

"Angel—" Diane looked sympathetically at her.

Angel peered ahead of herself, about to light her cigarette.

Diane said, "You know you'll have to put that out."

Reluctantly, Angel threw the cigarette down.

"Wait up! Hey, you all! Guys!" A girl's voice called from several yards below them. Angel squinted, discovering Chubby, heaving and panting, nevertheless jogging up the hill to catch up with them.

"I like being fat!" she cried loudly to no one in particular. "I really do. Catherine the Great was fat. No one made her jog. And what about Orson Welles?"

Diane and Angel's eyes met. Both of them attempted to stifle the gales of laughter that threatened to explode from them. "We shouldn't," Diane whispered, grabbing Angel's arm.

"But can we help it?" Angel asked.

Several minutes later, Chubby jogged past them, saying, "If I lose weight, I'll get flat-chested. Then what'll happen? I'll sue Camp Little Wolf! That's what I'll do!"

"How'd she get up here?" Angel asked, amazed.

"You never can tell, huh?" Diane said.

"Lots of men like fat women!" Chubby continued jogging. When she reached the top, she looked around. "Hey, where's everybody?"

Angel shook her head, grinning. Her dark eyes shone as she walked with Diane.

7

"WOULD you mind passing the bread," Cinder said frostily. "Puh-leez . . ." They sat across from each other at a long table.

Angel had grabbed several slices and heaped them on her plate, neglecting to pass the bread basket.

"Don't they teach you anything at home?" Cinder added, rolling her eyes. She grabbed the bread basket. "Jesus."

Angel continued eating, gulping her vegetable soup loudly. Every few moments, she glanced around self-consciously, noticing how much faster she ate than anybody else. The other girls had real manners, especially Ferris, who picked at her food daintily, chewing so you couldn't even tell there was anything in her mouth.

Both were with their own self-appointed teams. Ferris sat next to Cinder, then Carrots, Sunshine and some other girls Angel didn't know very well. On Angel's side of the table, it was Dana, Penelope and Chubby. Angel took some more bread.

"Puke!" Carrots cried, sipping a glass of milk. "I hate lukewarm milk. It tastes of cow balls."

Sunshine frowned. "Do you have to talk about things like that?" She took several pills with her juice. "Milk causes mucus," she said after swallowing. Then she dropped several more pills into the palm of her hand.

"Not according to Cleopatra," Dana remarked. "She bathed in milk." Dana leaned over the table to reach for the salt.

"P.U.! She must of stunk in warm weather," Penelope cried, wrinkling her nose.

"Who said you could speak, punk?" Angel demanded.

Penelope piped down, deferring to her.

"Drink," Sunshine told Ferris as she dropped a tablet into her glass. She patted her on the back.

"What is it?" Ferris asked, staring at her glass in the light.

"Ginseng. It'll make you sexy," Sunshine giggled.

"Did you see that?" Dana asked, poking Angel in the ribs.

"We're not going to need any false stimulants," Chubby insisted. "Right, Angel?"

She didn't answer.

Cinder was writing in a notebook when Miss Nickels walked past. She slipped her finger into her place and shut the book. "My journal," she said. "I write poetry."

"Oh, so creative," Miss Nickels approved. "Good girl."

Miss Nickels sat down at a nearby table with the other counselors, pointing with satisfaction to their table.

A high ponytail bobbed above their table. The girl gave Cinder some money. "Cabin C bets it all on her."

She opened the notebook to the page where her

finger kept her place. "Ferris?" Cinder asked, all business.

The girl nodded excitedly. "She doesn't have a chance," she added, peering at Angel.

"Okay, I've got it," Cinder said, jotting down this bet along with the others. "Ferris . . . Cabin C for Ferris."

Carrots and Sunshine cheered loudly while the girls of cabin C waved across the room at Ferris. She smiled broadly, enjoying the attention despite herself.

Dana slumped miserably in her chair. "It doesn't look good," she muttered.

All of a sudden, there was a confused clamor as six girls came running into the dining room. Titters and soft applause boomed throughout the room. The girls sported t-shirts with ANGEL painted on them. Dana cheered loudly. "HOORAY!" Chubby and Penelope joined in.

Angel hid her face in her hands, cracking up.

"We have to do that too!" Cinder cried jealously.

"Yeah," Carrots added. "I can draw the letters."

Gary Callahan grinned as he watched the action at their table. "They're up to something," he said. "I just know it."

In the recreation room, Cinder held Ferris' ankles as she did sit-ups. After the seventh one, she stopped. "Do I really have to do this?" she asked, wiping her forehead.

"Three more and then deep knee bends. Men are not turned on by flab," Cinder said. "Or cellulite."

On the other side of the room, Sunshine and Carrots were stenciling Ferris' name on t-shirts. They laughed as they worked. When Ferris finished her final sit-up, they held up one. "Hey, champ! How do you like it?"

Ferris laughed, shaking her head slowly. She finally felt like she was part of a group, that she was liked. But the contest worried her. Could she? With whom? She couldn't even imagine it. Then Gary's handsome face came to mind. Are you kidding, she scolded herself. Never!

"Okay, deep knee bends," Cinder called authoritatively.

Ferris gave her the hairy eyeball. "Do I have to?"

"To tighten your seat and the back of your thighs."

"What's wrong with them the way they are?" she asked.

"Come on!" Cinder barked. "I have better things to do with my life than stand around here."

"Look, it wasn't my idea," Ferris protested.

"Never mind!" Cinder cried, exasperated. Then she lowered her voice. "You know, I have my residual check on the line . . ." She paused. "Even if money doesn't mean very much to you."

Ferris winced visibly.

"It looks beautiful!" Sunshine cried. "What do you think?" Red spangles were glued to the letters on the t-shirt.

Ferris clapped her hands. "You both deserve Academy Awards!" Then she turned to Cinder. "Could you cut it out about the money thing? Okay?"

Cinder nodded reluctantly.

"Deep knee bends it will be," Ferris said, her muscles creaking as she lowered herself.

"Straight back!" Cinder ordered.

8

AT the lake next morning, Ferris lay sunning on a towel while some of the other girls swam. Chubby did laps from the pier to a rowboat which Penelope navigated. "Twelve!" she called. "Eight more to go."

"Come in!" Carrots called, grabbing her nose before plunging underwater. "It's wet."

"Nah!" Ferris said, shielding her eyes with her hand. She reapplied her sun screen, hoping that it would work and she wouldn't end up covered with red splotches. As she was about to lie down again, she saw Gary approaching her.

Something about him made Ferris feel dizzy, almost headachy whenever she saw him. Her stomach became a nest of butterflies and, half the time, she couldn't think of anything intelligent to say to him. But it was a pleasant, curious sensation.

"How you doing?" he asked, sitting down on the grass next to her. He wore a Columbia sweatshirt and cut-off jeans.

"Uh, fine," she said, tugging at the bottom of her

suit, embarrassed. Her body felt awkward, unwieldy, a stranger to her suddenly.

"You and Angel getting along?" he asked.

She nodded. "Sure. Well, sort of, uh, Mr. Callahan . . ."

"Yes, Miss Whitney," he grinned, teasing her.

Staring at her toes, she blurted, "Are you married?"

"No, are you?" He smiled warmly at her.

"No, of course not." She laughed, attempting to pull the shoulder straps of her suit. "What do you do—in the city?" She tried to make her voice sound older, experienced and worldly.

"I teach French at Roosevelt High."

"Wow!" Ferris exclaimed, all sophistication evaporating. "French is my favorite of all languages. *Allez-vous au cinéma français?*"

"*Oui. Êtes-vous?*"

She felt as if she might burst with excitement. His dark eyes seemed to penetrate her. She dropped her eyes shyly. "*Mais oui. J'ai vu 'Pardon Mon Affaire' deux fois.* I loved it!"

He laughed heartily, forgetting that Ferris was only fifteen. She was a lovely, cultivated young woman. He felt attracted to her.

"Your accent's impeccable," he commended her.

She grinned but her cheeks flushed at the compliment. "Thanks."

"Where'd you learn to speak so well?"

"Paris," Ferris said, leaning back as she relaxed with him.

"It figures . . ." he said, laughing.

"What?" she asked. "You can tell?" She felt embarrassed.

He looked at her. "Oh, it's just that it didn't sound like your high school French."

"I see," she said somewhat doubtfully.

"How long were you there?" he asked.

"Three years . . ."

As they spoke, she gazed out at the lake. She knew that Gary was watching her, that he noticed her changes of mood. She felt a bond with him, as if he could read into her mind and discover her most secret thoughts, that she wanted someone to know.

"Traveling can be rough sometimes," he said sympathetically. "Doesn't give a person time to really make friends . . ."

She turned longingly toward him. He ruffled her hair playfully as she had seen him do with the other girls. Suddenly she felt torn, completely exposed. She wanted to cover her body, flee somewhere and also, simultaneously, never leave this spot where her handsome counselor spoke French with her.

"I didn't mind," she said, bringing her knees to her chest protectively. "Sometimes it was weird . . . Thanksgiving. Did you know they don't have Thanksgiving in Paris?"

"Oh, is that so—"

"But the museums are real neat," she said, grinning.

"Where'll you go to school this year?"

"Here," she said. "Is Roosevelt High a private school?" she asked hopefully.

"Nope." He shook his head.

"Oh . . ." Her voice dropped in disappointment.

"Have to go to private school, huh?"

She nodded, feeling her face burn with embarrassment. "It's worse than that. Dad wants it to be all girls. Can you imagine that? God, I'm going to O.D. on females. You know what I mean?"

He laughed. "I don't know if I could ever feel that way myself—"

"Mr. Callahan, can I ask you something personal?" Ferris said, looking deeply into his eyes.

"Uh huh."

"What sign are you?"

"I thought you were going to ask something personal. Leo." He smiled.

"Honest?" she exclaimed excitedly.

"Are we supposed to be compatible?" he asked, teasing her.

"Oh, yes. Very!" She turned away. "Extremely!"

"Good," he said, beaming at her.

When their eyes met again, both began to laugh at the same time. "You're something else," Ferris said.

"So are you."

A girl ran past them, wearing an ANGEL t-shirt. Ferris shook her head. "I don't believe this," she muttered.

"Angel's got it made!" the girl called.

"What's that all about?" Gary asked, looking at Ferris. "I've seen some other girls. As a matter of fact, their t-shirts said FERRIS . . ." He scrutinized her. "Do you know anything about it?"

"Uh," she said, trying to be as truthful as possible, but her expression revealed that she was fabricating the story as she told it. "Uh, well, you see . . . it's this, uh, project—a science thing . . ." She grabbed her towel. Her sun screen fell to the ground. She picked it up, continuing. "Uh, sort of . . . you know, an experiment. Biology . . ."-She tried to meet his eyes. "Yes, that's it. Biology . . ." And it wasn't even a total lie, she told herself. Biology, it was. Birds and bees.

Gary smiled, helping her get her things. "Uh huh. None of my business, right?"

She started to add to her story, but midway decided to be truthful. "It's like a—no . . ." She looked at him. "You're right. I can't tell you about it."

"Don't worry about it." As he smiled, his eyes shone darkly.

"You've got the greatest eyes, Mr. Callahan!" Ferris suddenly cried, running away toward the woods. He watched her curiously, her winsome body with lovely legs. Then he shook his head—as if it were a definite no-no. But when Ferris turned to wave to him, he leaped into the air and waved with both arms.

On another side of the lake, a row of girls sat, binoculars to eyes, gazing across the lake. Mr. Lido stood nearby.

"I don't see anything," Chubby complained. "Not a single thing." Sunshine tried to help her.

"Point it toward the wharf over there," Dana said. "I am!"

"Well, then you must be blind," Cinder exclaimed. "Don't you see them?"

Angel put down her binoculars. "Who wants to see a bunch of guys skinny-dipping?"

"I do!" Chubby cried. "But I still can't see anything."

Dana looked at Angel. "This is important. Maybe you'll find someone who'll appeal to you."

"Not through binoculars, I won't."

"You want to win, don't you?" Dana pleaded.

"Oh, no!" Penelope, white with shock, put her binoculars down and started to walk away. "Forget it. Count me out."

"What's wrong?" Dana asked.

"Oh boy!" Chubby exclaimed. "I see what you mean! God, they're beautiful."

Dana picked up the binoculars and stared raptly across the lake. "Not bad at all," she muttered.

There were four boys, all in rosy birthday suits, diving from the pier, passing a Frisbee. One boy climbed the pier and prepared to dive. But first, he waved to the girls, shaking his hips like a hula dancer.

"Did you see that?" Chubby cried ecstatically.

" 'That unmatched form and feature of blown youth blasted with ecstasy. O, woe is me, to see what I have seen—see what I see . . .' " Dana recited.

"What are you mouthing off about now?" Angel demanded.

"Those were Ophelia's lines to Hamlet. It means he's cute. Don't you know anything?"

"I know one thing," she answered defensively. "That looking at a bunch of creeps skinny-dipping might turn you on—but I think it's crap."

"Did you girls see the robin?" Mr. Lido asked, hopping with excitement. "Unusual coloring, very unusual . . ."

"Oh, yes, Mr. Lido," Dana said. "Gorgeous." She continued to peer through the binoculars. "I think I see another bird. It's kind of pink—" She covered her mouth, cracking up.

"Where?" He raised his binoculars, squinting. When the naked boys came into his view, he gasped. "Oh!" Then he dropped the binoculars and took several steps away from the girls. "Hmm," he muttered, scratching his head. "Let's see if we can find any other interesting birds." He wandered absently into the trees.

"Poor man," Sunshine commented.

Cinder dropped her binoculars momentarily. "I told you Angel wasn't interested in the opposite sex."

"Bull," Angel said disgustedly. "I just don't get my kicks that way."

"Well, you can't get pregnant from looking," Chubby said.

Carrots put down her binoculars. "God, I hope not!"

Sunshine looked up. "Hey, what are they going to do about that?"

"What?"

"Protection," Sunshine declared.

"What do you mean?" Carrots asked innocently.

Dana studied her with suspicion. "Birth control, bozo," she explained. "Eight is too many. No bambinos."

"Oh," Carrots said. "I forgot about that part."

"Doesn't the guy take care of that?" Chubby asked. "What I read is that—"

"Do you believe everything you read?" Cinder demanded.

Angel scoffed. "They don't do shit since the pill."

"And how would you know?" Cinder asked. "You're even scared to look at a couple of naked guys."

"I am not."

"Guys!" Dana interrupted, raising her voice. "This is a serious impediment. What are we going to do?"

"How about the rhythm system?" Sunshine suggested.

"We only have a couple of weeks," Dana said.

"That's right," Carrots added. "But I thought it only takes a couple of minutes to"—she giggled—"you know."

"Will somebody help this girl?" Chubby asked. "Whew!"

Angel smiled as Carrots, looking confused, muttered, "That's something I'm sure of. It can't take weeks . . ."

Cinder ignored her. "Rubbers. We'll have to get them for the guys."

"Oh, yuck!" Carrots cried, her mouth dropping with revulsion. Everyone turned to look at her at the same time. "Are you sure you—"

"Well, one thing for sure," Cinder said. "We can't exactly go to the camp infirmary."

"Don't you think they're disgusting?" Carrots asked Sunshine. "You know, the way they're, uh—" She paused, glancing anxiously around herself. She had to say something. "They're so rubbery, and, uh" —her mind raced—"uh, and—uh, red . . ."

Sunshine peered seriously at her. "God, you must have been into some pretty kinky stuff . . ."

Carrots nodded happily.

9

"THE moral fabric has come undone in these, our chaotic times . . ." The priest's voice rose, warming to his sermon, permissiveness and sexual promiscuity among Christian youth. Eight girls in the back row sneaked out, one by one.

As Chubby waddled out, a wooden chair toppled over. "Damn!" she whispered.

"There's been a loss of—" He stopped, peering intently over the pulpit. Although his eyes flashed like brimstone, he was nearsighted, so he continued sternly, "A serious loss to all of us, young and old alike . . ."

They ran as fast as they could, pulling each other by arms and sleeves, covering their faces so as not to laugh, cough, scream with hysteria. When they reached the dirt road where the yellow Camp Little Wolf bus was parked, Carrots jumped in the air and made a whooping sound. "We did it!" she shrieked. "Freedom!"

"The way he was going on, I thought I'd die of boredom."

"Yeah, me too."

"And this is supposed to be our vacation."

Angel and Cinder boosted Penelope up to the open bus window. As they began to push her through, she protested. "I'll never get in. It's too—"

Angel cut her off. "Shut it."

Penelope landed on the driver's seat. She smiled, swinging open the door. Everyone piled on the bus.

"Can you really get this started?" Sunshine asked.

"I need a hairpin," Angel said, sitting at the wheel.

"Here," Cinder said, giving her a barrette with rhinestones.

"I can't use this," Angel muttered. "Anybody?"

Dana passed her a bobbypin. "Can you use this?"

"I'll try." Angel stuck the bobbypin into the ignition, jiggling it in one direction, then the other but there was no sound. She tried angling the pin. Not even a peep.

"How about a paper clip?" Penelope called.

"What are you doing with a paper clip?" Cinder asked.

Penelope dug into her Kiss t-shirt and rummaged around. "I figured it might come in handy sometime. Besides," she glanced at herself, "it keeps the paper in place."

Angel opened the paper clip and worked the top of it into the ignition, turning it gingerly. "Here goes nothing," she said as she pulled it out slowly, turning it. There was a soft rumble. The motor started working. "I don't believe it," Ferris cried.

"Yay!" Chubby screamed. "You did it!"

Angel grinned, returning the paper clip to Penelope. "So your stuff doesn't fall out," she said.

Penelope worked it down into her t-shirt, attaching it to the strap of her training bra. "There. I knew it'd come in handy."

They took the back roads so as not to be discovered, past farms where cows lay sleepily in clusters on the grassy hills. There were sharp turns which Angel easily mastered except for one which sent all of the girls reeling from one side of the bus to the other.

"Hey, take it easy!" Dana called.

"I'm too young to die," Carrots said, clutching her throat.

Angel stuck her arm out of the window, taking it all in happily. The last time she hot-wired a car, it was her mother's and did she ever get pissed. Today Angel wasn't alone. She liked that. And the sun shone as it never did on her block.

Ferris sat quietly, her knuckles white from clutching her seat. But as the girls around her sang rock and roll songs, she joined them, relaxing. ". . . Talkin' about bad girls . . . ," she sang.

Cinder sat down next to her. "I advise you to choose an experienced man," she said softly.

Ferris looked at her. "I will . . ." Then she confided, "I already have . . ." Her face flushed magenta. "Well, sort of—"

"You have!" Carrots exclaimed, joining them. "Who?"

"You know who," Ferris said, smiling amorously.

"Who?" Sunshine asked. "Oh. You don't mean—"

Ferris nodded. "Gary Callahan."

"But he's so *old*," Sunshine said.

Cinder was delighted. "He's perfect. He really is." She patted Ferris on the back. "Fine choice, really fine . . ."

Carrots looked nauseated. "I can't imagine having sexual intercourse with him."

"Do you have to put it so crudely?" Ferris demanded.

"And he's so hairy," Carrots added.

The bus jerked as it hurtled up a mountain road. Dana grabbed the back of the seats, stumbling down the aisle to the front of the bus. Angel glanced at her in the rear-view mirror.

"You know, Ferris already has her target," she told Angel.

"What?" Angel asked, turning to Dana.

"Watch the road!" she screamed.

Angel stepped on the brake, tires squealing as she just narrowly missed the side of the mountain. The bus swerved and broke off a tree branch.

"God help me!" Chubby shouted, grabbing Cinder.

Cinder threw her off. "Will you cool it! Angel!"

Sunshine closed her eyes, chanting softly.

"What are you doing?" Carrots asked.

Sunshine opened her eyes. "Meditating."

"Okay, I'll talk but you keep your eyes on the road," Dana said. "Ferris has someone, so you better move fast. I bet my whole summer's allowance on you." She pointed to her.

"I'll win," Angel said. "Stop bugging me."

"Just remember, a man reaches his sexual peak at seventeen. From then on it . . ." Her finger dropped limply. "It's downhill. We'll have to find you a horny thirteen-year-old."

"If you don't mind, Dana, I'll do the choosing. Hey, watch it!" she screamed at a truck in front of her.

Stepping hard on the accelerator, Angel built up speed. As she was about to pass the truck, it raced ahead of her, covering the windshield with a thick blanket of dust.

"I can't see anything!" Angel cried angrily. "Damn bus."

She put the bus in neutral, coming to a screeching halt.

"What's going on?"

"Is it all over?" Sunshine asked, her eyes closed.

"Someone get their ass out and clean the windshield," Angel called. When no one stirred, she screamed, "Well?"

"With what?" Carrots asked.

"I don't know. Use your imagination."

Cinder rushed up to the front. "What the hell's taking so long? We can't keep the bus all day."

Angel pointed to the windshield.

"Oh."

"If I take my foot off the gas, I'm afraid it won't start again."

"Never mind," Cinder said. "I'll do it."

"I'll help," Ferris offered.

Cinder slipped off her black t-shirt, standing in only her flesh-colored lace bra. Then she stepped out of the bus.

A white Winnebago camper which passed them suddenly braked and backed up—to make sure that it was not a hallucination and that they had actually seen a lovely dark-haired girl cleaning the windshield, topless.

Cinder turned to them, posing brazenly so that her lush cleavage spilled over. "How do you like it?"

"Look at that!" a freckled teenager cried.

His mother grabbed him abruptly. "That isn't a nice girl. No nice girl would stand like that," she said. "Don't look, Shermy."

"But she isn't naked," he said.

All the girls waved from the bus, screaming, "So long, sucker!"

When the windshield was cleared of most of the

dust, Cinder shook her t-shirt and then put it back on. Carrots and Sunshine applauded. She sat down.

"That was great!"

"Did you catch that creepy guy?"

"Oh, was he ugly."

Carrots leaned over the seat, asking, "Didn't you feel kind of funny with that guy looking at you?"

Cinder ran her hands through her hair. "What have I got to hide?"

Dana stared jealously at her.

Carrots shook her head vehemently. "I guess so. I mean, my brothers have seen me in my underwear and all. But Cinder, I'd never have the nerve to do that."

Sitting next to her, Ferris thought: neither would I. Cinder was such a curious mixture of courage, spunk and a spiteful mean streak. Yet she admired her attitude. She'd do anything she wanted and didn't care what anyone else thought.

The bus started again. Angel honked the horn three times.

"Onward!" Dana called. "Let's get this show on the road."

"Prophylactics, here we come!"

10

Somewhere in the nowhere of a narrow country road, the kidnapped, hot-wired yellow CAMP LITTLE WOLF bus rattled along, past trailers and barns and a house that still had all its Christmas decorations and lights, horses that grazed sleepily near the road while crows sat on wooden posts. They passed a railroad crossing and continued, stopping only to allow a boy to cross the road who was wheeling a youngster in a red wagon with a yelping spotted dog running behind him.

"Do you have any place in mind?" Dana asked after several minutes, sitting next to Angel.

"I'm looking for a gas station," Angel said. "We haven't passed any that were open." She peered ahead.

"Oh," Dana said. "What are we going to do if we don't find one?"

"Don't worry," Angel muttered.

"No one said it was going to be such a long trip," Chubby complained. "I've got to tinkle anyway."

"Tinkle?" Dana repeated incredulously. "I haven't heard that since kindergarten."

"Does anybody know where we are?" Ferris asked.

"Lost," Cinder answered. "And we're really going to catch hell when we get back. Not that I really care. Can you just see Miss Nickels' face?"

"Spare me," Sunshine said.

"What a puss," Carrots added. "If I looked like that, I'd have myself put to sleep." She closed her eyes and fell back on the seat.

Chubby cracked up. "Please don't make me laugh."

"I need a john too, by the way," Sunshine said softly.

"Hey!" Angel called. "I think there's something coming up."

"You're right," Dana said, squinting out of the window. "Land ho! I feel like Columbus."

"What's Middleville?" Cinder asked. "God, the sticks."

"Don't sneeze or you'll miss it."

"Where's the gas station around here?"

"Probably the same place as the luncheonette."

They passed a decrepit-looking movie theater that was playing *Rocky II*. Two pimply-faced teenage boys stood in front of it.

"Did any of you see that?" Carrots asked, looking up.

"I don't like him," Penelope said. "He's too macho."

"I don't know," Cinder said, posing dreamily. "I wonder if Robbie misses me . . ."

Angel turned to her. "He probably misses your boobs. That's all."

"One day," Cinder declared snottily, "you too may grow into a sex object."

A post office, laundromat, diner and grocery store

came into view, and then finally a small Shell station. The girls cheered.

Carrots interrupted. "Hey, guys, do you really think they'll have any—here?" She looked outside. "It seems so quiet around here."

"They don't only do it in big cities," Dana said, fixing her glasses.

"I don't know about that," Carrots insisted.

Angel lit a cigarette as she stared out at the sun-baked street. It was so quiet that if someone coughed, the whole town would hear. She brought the bus to a smooth stop in front of the gas station.

"Hooray, Angel!" Chubby called, climbing out of the bus.

"Coming?" Cinder asked snottily.

"Bug off," Angel murmured.

Even though some of the girls were pains, especially Cinder, who walked around with her reflection plastered before her eyes, Angel had to admit that the summer was okay. She leaned back in her seat, enjoying the quiet which was so unlike her neighborhood, where you never knew if someone was going to try to rip you off or what. It felt strange.

"We're going to look for rubbers," Sunshine said brightly.

"Well, they don't grow, you know," Angel answered, not opening her eyes.

"I bet they don't have any," Carrots still insisted. "Only five people live in this town and they're all senile."

They all ran to a red-painted door which said MEN. Cinder tried the door.

"It's locked," she said. "Damn it."

"You're screwed," Chubby told Ferris.

"Not yet, she isn't," Dana insisted, throwing all her weight against the door. It didn't budge.

"There must be a way," Ferris said, looking around.

Angel opened her eyes. "What's the problem?" she called, sticking her head out of the window. "Oh . . ." She leaned out farther. "What about up there?"

Angel pointed to a small window that was open above the men's room. "We'd never fit," Ferris said, shaking her head.

"No," Angel agreed. "But that little squirt—" She looked at Penelope. "She could fit in."

Penelope was about to take off when Carrots and Cinder rushed to stop her. "I can't," she screamed. "I'm afraid of heights. Really! No!"

They boosted her onto Cinder's shoulders.

"I'm scared," she whined.

"We won't let you fall," Carrots assured her. "Don't worry. We've got you."

"Now stand up, Penelope," Cinder said, standing against the door. "Come on."

She hesitated, looking around herself. "Do I have to?" Then she stood up slowly on Cinder's shoulders, her legs wobbling. "I'm going to kill myself. I just know it."

"Go on, hurry!"

"Penelope—"

"Oh, okay." She reached for the window. "I got it!"

Just then, a car pulled into the station. Penelope turned around, her expression aghast, so frightened that she scurried up to the window sill and pulled herself in. She disappeared inside.

"Come on," Dana cried. "Let's get out of here."

"But we can't leave Penelope in there," Ferris protested.

"Hey, Penelope!" Carrots called.

"Pipsqueak!"

"What's happening in there?"

"Let's split," Dana pleaded. "We can come back for her in a few minutes."

"I don't know."

"Penelope!" they called.

"Now what are we going to do?" Chubby demanded. "Suppose they're cops?"

The car door opened. A young man got out. The girls huddled together in front of the men's room, guarding the door.

Angel slipped back into her seat on the bus, just in case there was some trouble. She watched the blue Ford in her rear-view mirror.

11

THE young man in a sexy muscle shirt and jeans, carrying a beer can, headed for the men's room. "Hi, girls!" he called, grinning broadly. "Nice day."

One by one they abandoned the door, walking slowly.

"Don't worry, we're still here," Carrots called softly inside. She ran to catch up with the others.

As he passed the bus, Angel looked him over appreciatively. He was really something. About six feet tall, at least, and his body was lean and muscular. He weaved slightly as he walked. That's the one, Angel told herself. She turned to check his car and noticed a girl sitting at the steering wheel.

He turned the doorknob of the men's room. "When ya gotta pee, ya gotta pee. Right?" He hiccoughed loudly.

"Uh, somebody's in there," Ferris said nervously.

"Oh, okay." He leaned up against the wall, smiling as the sunlight hit his face. Soon he crossed his legs, staring at the door. He looked as if he had some difficulty holding on.

"Too much beer," he commented, shaking his head.

Angel lit a cigarette and walked over to where he stood. "You live around here?" she asked.

"Who me?" He looked around, trying to concentrate.

"Yeah, you. I know where I live."

He hiccoughed again. "Excuse me . . . Where do I live? Oh, yeah. I'm from Camp Tomahawk."

Standing out of his angle of vision, Carrots mimed a pair of binoculars, watching them. Angel nodded indifferently while the boy, clutching himself in agony, stared at the men's room door with yearning and anticipation.

Cinder snickered.

"Maybe we should knock and see if he's all right —in there," he suggested hopefully.

Ferris turned to him. "Oh, no. We just flew in from Tijuana. We warned him not to drink the water. And you see what happens?" She smiled mischievously. "Water everywhere . . ."

"Right!" the girls added. "He'll probably be in there forever. I hope it isn't dysentery—"

"Just Tijuana revenge . . ."

Carrots whispered to Sunshine, "What's taking so long?"

She shrugged her shoulders. "Who knows?"

"Where'd you get the car?" Angel asked, dropping her voice.

"Car? Oh, I borrowed it."

"What about the girl?"

He looked at her, grinning smartly. "She came with the car." He put his ear to the door. "Are you sure someone's in there?"

"Oh, yes!" a chorus of voices shrieked. "Definitely!"

Inside of the men's room, Penelope was frantic. She had dropped six quarters into the prophylactic machine and nothing had happened. So she began to bang on the machine with her fist, checking the coin return slot. "Darn!" she cried. "Now what am I going to do? Hey, fellows," she groaned.

"So what's your name?" Angel asked.

"Me?" He recrossed his legs desperately.

"I know my name," she said, propped against the wall.

"Yeah?" He turned to look at her. "What is it?"

"Angel." She raised her eyebrows and jutted her chin out. "But don't let the name fool you."

"Who's fooling who?" he asked.

Angel laughed. He leaned over to her, smiling, almost losing his balance and falling on top of her. "Excuse me!"

"You're drunk," she said, shaking her head.

"You're cute." His eyes twinkled as he smiled at her.

She stopped laughing and began to feel embarrassed. "You still haven't told me your name." Angel stared down at her feet.

"It's Randy."

She nodded. "Hi."

"But don't let the name fool you," he said, his eye catching hers suggestively.

Ferris frowned as she observed this. She mustn't let Angel make progress. So she knocked on the men's room door.

Penelope gave a startled gasp. She was standing on the sink, trying to shake the prophylactic machine. All of a sudden, there was a loud crash, bang and a cry of delight.

"What's that?" Randy demanded.

"Maybe they did what they had to do," Carrots said.

A moment later, the door opened and Penelope stood there, her face beaming. She held the prophylactic machine in her arms.

"I don't believe it!" Ferris cried.

"Now that's what I call coming prepared!" Dana added.

Everyone laughed and applauded Penelope. "You did it, kid!"

"Where's the party?" Randy asked as he darted into the bathroom. "Right on, ladies!" He cheered, shutting the door.

"See ya again, Randy!" Angel called.

She helped the girls boost Penelope and the prophylactic machine up into the bus. Then the rest got on and Angel revved the motor. Soon they were on their way.

"Camp Tomahawk, huh?" Angel said to herself. "You just better not have that dishwater blonde around the next time." He was really something.

Several miles down the road, the bus began to slow down. Angel stepped on the gas. The bus conked out completely.

Ferris ran to the front. "What happened?" Then she noticed that the fuel tank reading was empty. "I don't suppose it ever occurred to you to check the fuel gauge."

"The gas station was closed, dummy."

Dana joined them. "So where's the nearest service station?"

"That was it," Cinder said.

"Shit."

They stared ahead of themselves at the road.

"There probably isn't a phone anywhere around here," Chubby said.

"What the hell are we going to do?"

"We could eat the rubbers," Penelope suggested brightly.

"Let's get out and walk," Angel said, opening the door.

"Do you know where we are?" Cinder demanded.

"No, but we'll find out."

"Oh, sure."

"Maybe someone'll give us a lift."

"Dream on . . ."

"This is the pits," Chubby complained as they filed out of the bus. "I mean, the absolute pits."

"You are the pits . . ."

"So are you—"

"Your mother."

"I can hardly walk in these," Cinder cried, hobbling in her three-inch-heel sandals.

"Bitch, bitch, bitch," Angel declared. "Can anybody think of anything else to do?"

As they traipsed down the narrow road, leaving the yellow bus behind them, they passed an old cemetery. "That's where we'll probably end up," Dana muttered. They took turns carrying the prophylactic machine.

"This weighs a ton," Carrots moaned.

"There's got to be enough rubbers in here," Angel said, holding up the other end on her back, "to supply the whole U.S. Navy." She shifted her weight forward.

"Mosquitoes!" Dana cried, swatting her arm. "I hate mosquitoes!"

"Will you watch it!" Cinder muttered as Chubby tripped, bumping into her.

"It was an accident. There are all these pebbles—"

"We'll never get back."

"Shaddup."

"Why should I?"

"It could be worse," Ferris remarked. "There could be rapists on the road like in *The Virgin Spring*—"

"Did you have to say that?" Chubby demanded, peering into the woods on both sides of the road. "Cree-py . . ." she shuddered.

"I wouldn't worry," Cinder said snottily. "That is, if I looked like you."

"Stuff it."

"I can't walk in these." Cinder slipped off her shoes and buckled them together so she could throw them over her shoulder. She took a tentative step, then another.

"Does anybody know any ghost stories?" Carrots asked. "Maybe we could tell some and that way, by the time we got finished, we'd be closer and—"

"I wish I had taken another multiple vitamin," Sunshine fretted. "And a little extra iron . . ."

"It's like being on a desert," Penelope said, staring ahead of herself. "There's nothing out here. No food, water. Maybe we'll see a mirage—"

"Who told you that you could speak?" Angel asked.

When they heard the honking of a horn behind them, they spun around, shouting, "Hey, you! How about a ride!" They waved and howled. "Please give us a lift!"

An old truck stacked with chickens in wire cages passed them by, without even slowing down. A cloud of dust settled over them.

"The chickenshit."

"I bet it's not that far," Ferris said. "It looks really familiar around here."

"That's because it all looks the same."

"Ugh!" Ferris exclaimed when it was her turn to carry the prophylactic machine. "Do we really need all these? There's enough here to solve India's population problem."

"My dear," Cinder said, carrying the other end. "It's not *we* who need them but you and—" She pointed to Angel. "Her."

"But so many?"

"Well, you need some to practice on," Carrots interjected. "So you can put it in right . . . I mean, I didn't know how to put it in at first." As she saw the other girls around her groan, she asked, "Hey, guys?"

"Cut the gab," Angel said finally. "Everybody move their butts." A long hill was in front of them and they were at the bottom.

It was dark when they reached the outskirts of Camp Little Wolf. Never before did any place seem so wonderful to them. Dana wanted to kiss the grass. The glow of the lights in the cabins seemed like salvation.

They were all exhausted, mosquito-bitten and incredibly starved. No one uttered a word as they sneaked across the baseball field, past the dining room and recreation hall, until they finally, miraculously, opened the screen door and tiptoed into cabin A.

12

NEXT morning, the girls stood on the food line
like the living dead. Eyelids droopy, feet sore, bodies
fatigued, they stumbled and supported their weight
on the counter.

"I have fourteen mosquito bites," Dana informed
them. "Look at this." She rolled up her sleeves. "I
couldn't sleep."

"I've got at least that many," Carrots added.
"Probably more." Her pale freckled skin, including
her face, had pink puffy spots all over it. She took a
plate of sunnyside-up eggs.

Over the loudspeaker, the Camp Little Wolf news
report blared. "The girls of cabin C beat the pants off
of cabin B yesterday in a slambang volleyball game,
winning twenty-five to eighteen." Cabin C stood up
at their table, applauding themselves. Cabin B booed
loudly. The girls on the food line ignored the report.

"I just gained two inches in my breasts," Chubby
said. "I measured before." She smiled groggily.

"That's flab, not breast," Cinder responded.

"And now for our Happy Hour News . . ." the report continued.

Dana peered over the counter at the eggs frying on the grill and made a face. "Eggs have been known to cause infertility in women . . ."

"Some eggs, dear?" the woman in the white uniform behind the counter asked.

"Never!" she exclaimed. "Wheatena, please, with a little calamine lotion . . ." her voice trailed off as she scratched a cluster of bites on her elbow. "Darn!"

"Huh?" the woman said, looking sternly at her.

"With honey, please."

Carrots stared at the prune juice. "Yuck!" she muttered. "Bug juice."

"Mac Soblinski, owner of Mac's Shell gas station in Middleville . . ."

Ferris tensely poked Cinder with her elbow. "Listen to this," she whispered.

"What I wouldn't do for a Mac burger," Chubby sighed.

"Shhh!" Angel exclaimed, listening intently.

". . . reported a theft of—" The news reporter chuckled. "You're not going to believe this, kids. A prophylactic machine was stolen from the men's room at his gas station."

"That's us!" Carrots gasped. "Wow, we're famous!"

"Shut up, stupid!" Angel said, grabbing her roughly by the arm. "Why don't you tell the whole world, asshole?"

"And Mac Soblinski has told us that he's offering a reward for its safe recovery. Good luck, Mac, hope you get your prophylactic machine back." Some soft rock began to play. All the girls stood on the food line, as if transfixed.

"Move!" Cinder called, poking Penelope. "My feet are killing me." She took a small container of milk and a bowl of oatmeal and hobbled self-consciously to a table in the back.

Chubby loaded her tray with two plates of fried eggs, several slices of toast and a big glass of chocolate milk.

"I feel as if my equilibrium has been upset," Penelope complained, taking her tray of corn flakes and milk.

"Here," Sunshine said, passing her a pill. "You might be low on B."

"Hey, maybe we could get the reward!" Carrots whispered excitedly to Ferris, who walked sleepily to the table, carrying a tray with only cereal and milk on it.

"But we're the ones who stole the machine," she murmured. "I hope they don't know anything——"

Angel nudged her in the back with her tray, sneering, "Well, if everyone keeps gabbing, somebody's gonna know."

Ferris turned around, shooting Angel a pissed look.

All the other chairs at the table were taken, so Angel and Ferris sat down next to each other.

"Excuse me," Ferris said, leaning forward.

Angel was about to reach across the table for the salt but remembered her manners. "Somebody pass the salt, huh," she said, her foot tapping with impatience.

"My, my," Cinder remarked. "Emily Post reincarnated."

Angel ignored her, standing up and grabbing the salt shaker. As she sat down, she accidentally knocked against Ferris' elbow. Her spoon fell loudly to the floor.

Angel looked around, embarrassed. But she tried to cover it up. "So sorry," she said overly sweetly.

Ferris bent down to retrieve her spoon. Thinking that Angel had pushed her deliberately, she retaliated by bumping into Angel, causing her glass of milk to spill. "Oh, gosh!" she exclaimed innocently. "How awful!"

The other girls had stopped eating and were watching to see what the next move would be.

"That's okay," Angel said good-naturedly. "It was an accident."

Angel went for her napkin, shoving the rest of the milk into Ferris' lap. Her expression was amused. The girls around them began to giggle.

"Will you look at that?" Ferris said, smiling. "Sometimes these things just can't be helped, I guess." She spilled her milk over Angel's t-shirt.

Angel grabbed Sunshine's orange juice and splashed it on Ferris. "Have some vitamin C."

"My goodness," Ferris exclaimed, taking her bowl of corn flakes and dumping its contents over Angel's head.

Angel wiped her face, grinning. She bent over and grabbed Dana's Wheatena. "It's really delicious," she remarked as she put the bowl on Ferris' head.

Soon they were pelting each other with salt, sugar, pepper and anything they could find on the table. The other girls threw pieces of dry cereal at each other. When they ran out of things, Angel ran to another table, returning with ketchup and mustard.

"Oh, no!" Carrots squealed.

Angel twisted the cap off of the ketchup. Ferris armed herself with Gulden's mustard. They laughed.

"I can't believe how immature both of you are," Cinder said, looking above it all.

When a pancake landed on her face, she peeled it off furiously. Everyone else cracked up. Angel reached over and poured some ketchup on Ferris'. head.

"Ugh, grosso!" Chubby shrieked. "It looks like blood."

Ferris touched the top of her head and glanced at her hand which was covered with ketchup. She nodded self-contentedly, then stuck her fingers in the Gulden's, wiping them on Angel's jeans.

"It's so *you*," she said, giggling. "Yellow is really your color."

"Oh, yeah!" Angel scooped up one of Carrot's sunnyside-up eggs and flung it at Ferris. It landed squarely on her cheek, the yolk dripping down her face.

"Guys!" Sunshine called, looking anxiously around. "Every time they eat meat, this happens."

Wiping her face with the back of her hand, Ferris picked up a glass of prune juice. Just as she was about to spray Angel with it, Carrots cried, "Here comes Diane. She's gonna kill us!" Their counselor walked down the aisle toward their table.

Gingerly, Ferris put the prune juice down. Everyone became silent, picking up their flatware and starting to eat. They pretended to not be aware of the food splattered on the table and all around them.

"What's happened here?" Diane demanded, looking from Ferris to Angel, then at the other girls who were only partly covered with Wheatena, corn flakes, milk, eggs, ketchup and mustard.

"What do you mean?" Dana asked innocently.

She shook her head. "If Miss Nickels sees this . . . Okay, cabin A has to clean this mess up. Got it?"

The girls nodded in unison.

As soon as she left their table, a strip of bacon went boomeranging across the room, right past Miss Nickels' beak. She shrieked with horror.

13

Miss Nickels' office had posters of the Sierra Madres and a Greek island and several charts of ideal weights, male and female, according to height and size of frame. There were cactus plants on the window sill and her whistle hung on a nail near the calendar, which had a photograph of Eleanor Roosevelt with the caption, Women in Leadership.

Cinder entered, taking a seat quietly. Ferris, Carrots and Sunshine followed. Dana ducked in, sitting down behind Ferris. Angel and Chubby were the last ones. As each girl entered, Miss Nickels clicked her tongue disapprovingly. She sat at her desk, holding a pencil in her hand.

Finally, when they were all seated, she leaned forward. She peered at them crossly, so infuriated that her eyes twitched.

"Never in all my years at Camp Little Wolf," she began, rising slowly, "never has anything so disgusting and unladylike occurred in our dining room, a place where people eat . . ."

She walked closer to them. Sunshine moved her chair backwards, frightened.

"You!" She pointed to her. Sunshine gave a startled gasp. "How could you throw food around like that? Don't you know about—about, uh, the Cambodian refugees?"

As Sunshine was about to answer, white with consternation, Miss Nickels turned to Carrots. "And you. Have you ever been hungry? I bet you never missed a dinner in your life." She confronted Chubby, who was biting her bottom lip so as not to laugh. "What about you?" Chubby sobered up immediately, looking obediently at the camp head. "You were throwing food around, weren't you?"

Chubby shook her head vehemently. "Oh, no. Not me."

"And you?" Miss Nickels stopped in front of Ferris, who was in the midst of knotting the bottom of her t-shirt. Ferris nodded guiltily.

Miss Nickels continued, past Cinder and Dana. When she came to Angel, she put her hands on her hips. "You," she said. "You look like the trouble-maker."

Angel sucked her teeth, not answering.

"The leader of this ring of desperadoes. What do you say?"

"I didn't do nothing," Angel mumbled.

Miss Nickels pointed to the yellow mustard stains on her jeans. "Maybe you just haven't learned to eat without making a mess all over yourself."

Carrots giggled nervously.

Miss Nickels spun around, demanding of Carrots, "What's so funny?"

She looked down. "Nothing, Miss Nickels. I was just, uh, clearing my, uh, throat."

Angel's eyes were dark and furious. She had always known it would come to this. If there was some trouble, she'd be blamed for it. Well, she had had enough of this place. She didn't care if they sent her home. She waited to see what Miss Nickels would do next. She stared out the window.

"Ladies, I know that one single bad influence can sometimes turn a whole group bad. Is that what happened?" She directed her question to Ferris. "A rotten apple in the barrel?"

Panic gripped at Ferris' chest. She looked around, from Cinder to Carrots to Sunshine, Dana and Chubby. Although Angel stared impassively, her body trembled.

"Well?" Miss Nickels said, picking up the sheet with the list of the girls' names. "Ferris Whitney, right?"

She nodded self-consciously.

Miss Nickels smiled. "I know that a girl from such a background as yours would never—uh, do such a thing." She shook her head. "I was impressed by your parents at the interview. Such refined people. Miss Whitney, dear—?"

Ferris took a deep breath, blurting her words out angrily. "It wasn't anybody's fault. Angel didn't do anything I didn't do."

Angel turned to her, her eyes wide with disbelief. Ferris wouldn't look at Angel, afraid that she might burst into tears, crack up, she didn't know what.

"That's right," Dana added. "Miss Nickels, it, uh, just happened."

"Yeah," Carrots interjected. "Just like that."

"There was a full moon last night," Sunshine suggested.

"Enough!" Miss Nickels screamed. "That's it! I've heard more than enough. Cabin A is docked from all social activities this week and there'll be silent suppers too. Until you can learn to act like ladies, not hooligans." She stormed out of her office.

When they were outside, Angel walked briskly past Ferris. "You didn't have to do that," she said. "Not for my benefit anyway. I don't give a damn what happens." She brushed a strand of hair out of her face. Receiving pity was not exactly her bag.

Ferris caught up to her, saying, "Don't worry. I didn't do it because of you. I just couldn't stand her."

Angel shot her a doubtful glance.

"Did you see her face when we said that?" Dana asked.

"Are you kidding!" Carrots exclaimed. "That's not a face. It's rat poison." They burst into nervous giggles.

Ferris and Angel walked back together to their cabin, silently. The sky had grown dark and the large weeping willow waved its leafy branches.

Just before reaching the cabin, Angel turned away, muttering under her breath, "Thanks."

Ferris heard it and grinned.

"But it doesn't change anything," Angel insisted. "Don't get the wrong idea, because I didn't ask you to, you know."

"Oh, I wouldn't think of it," Ferris assured her, detecting a softness as if Angel's hard exterior were melting.

14

THE activity on a glorious July afternoon was berry-picking. Diane led the girls on the road outside of the camp grounds, pointing out various flowers and mushrooms. Ferris walked with her, laughing happily as they spotted a rabbit.

The sun turned everything—bushes, leaves, grass —a brilliant emerald green that reminded Angel of *The Wizard of Oz,* which she had once watched on a neighbor's color TV. It was *that* green. Clapping an empty coffee can against her side, she dawdled behind Dana, Chubby and Penelope.

"When are you going to do something?" Dana demanded impatiently.

Angel looked up, surprised. "What are you mouthing off about now?"

"You know." Dana wiggled her third finger in the palm of her hand obscenely.

"I told you," Angel said. "I've got someone."

"What are you going to do?" Dana asked. "Wait for him to ask you to the junior prom?" She put her hands on her hips.

"I'll do it when I'm ready."

"Ferris has daily contact with her"—Chubby paused, smiling lecherously—"her lover."

"They're not lovers yet," Angel said, shaking her head.

"They will be if you don't move your ass," Dana insisted.

"Okay, already," she muttered, kicking a brown stone on the ground. It rolled several feet ahead of them.

Cinder, passing them briskly, called, "Will you watch it! Somebody could get hurt."

Angel ignored her.

"Don't forget," Penelope added, walking next to her. "We have all those rubbers that I almost killed myself to get."

Angel pushed her playfully. "Did you ask permission to speak?"

"Quit it," she said, falling forward. "Hey, blueberries!" She pointed to a bush by her sneaker that was fat with tiny blueberries. "Look, there're hundreds of them!"

The girls kneeled down with their coffee cans, picking the berries. "Do you think we'll have enough for blueberry pie?" Chubby asked. Her can was empty. She had eaten all the berries she'd gathered earlier.

Cinder caught up to the front of the line. She wore a large straw hat, coolie-style, satin shorts and a t-shirt with rhinestones spelling Studio 54. "I'll lend you my bathing suit for later," she whispered in Ferris' ear.

"I don't need it," Ferris began, glancing down at her own short-sleeved shirt and white tennis shorts. No matter what, she always ended up looking so pure and proper. It was disgusting. She turned to Cinder, "On second thought . . ."

"I'll give it to you when we get back," she answered, adjusting her hat as she walked away.

"What was that all about?" Diane asked.

"Nothing important." She paused, staring curiously at her counselor. "Can I ask you something?"

"Sure." Diane stopped.

"Uh, it's sort of personal." Ferris covered her chest with crossed arms as if she could hide her embarrassment. "Does making love help the complexion?" It was extremely difficult for her to talk about sex, but she needed to know some things before she embarked on her own experience. "Cinder said it was filled with vitamin E."

"Oh?" Diane said, somewhat astonished.

Ferris stammered. "You know, their stuff . . . What I want to know is whether when you, uh—do it—afterward, does your skin clear up?" Diane smiled, looking sympathetic while Ferris struggled. "Am I getting too personal? You're a counselor and older, I kind of thought you might know about—"

"I'm just," Diane replied, "just, I guess, surprised. You see, I'm supposed to keep you all busy so you don't think about those kinds of things." Her eyes met Ferris'. "Like sex."

"Lately that's all anybody ever talks about," Ferris said wryly.

"I really . . ." Diane began, her expression both understanding and quite amused. "I didn't expect it and I don't know what to say to you." She scratched her head perplexedly.

"Could you tell me what some of the aftereffects are?"

"What do you mean?" Diane looked confused.

"When you've—you know . . ." Ferris smiled tensely.

"Oh, you lost me there," Diane said. "You make sex sound like some kind of disease."

"It kind of is." Ferris stopped, her words falling all over each other as she tried to express herself. "I mean, before—I used to think about kissing a lot." Her face turned the color of blueberry dye. "I did and it was perfect, you know what I mean?" She scrutinized Diane.

"That it was romantic?" she asked.

"Yeah. Like The Kiss by Rodin and that was, uh, sort of the end. Now . . ." Ferris hesitated, eating a blueberry from her can. "Just suppose it happened to me. Would I be different afterward?"

"In a way," Diane said, choosing her words carefully. "It would really depend upon the kind of relationship you were—" She smiled uncomfortably at Ferris. "This is hard—"

Ferris grinned. "You're telling me?"

"Let me see," Diane continued, removing a bobbypin from her hair and repinning it. "If . . . you're not involved with the person—" She turned to Ferris suddenly, studying her. "You're not involved now, you?"

"No," she said. "Not exactly."

"We're talking about the future, right?"

Ferris nodded. "Sure. Tomorrow or the day after—" she teased. "Next week . . ."

"Don't do it until you're in love," Diane said, her voice growing serious, as she thought of her own first time.

"But if I'm in love," Ferris asked. "Then you'd think it'd be all right?"

Diane clutched her by the shoulders, eyeball to eyeball. "Yes, but later, Ferris. When you're older and, uh, really know what you're doing—" Her expression revealed concern.

"I thought you were modern," Ferris answered. "I am fifteen."

"Going on twenty-five." Diane laughed at herself. "I thought I was modern too. But more in the category of eighteen, not fifteen. It seems so young— for that." She shrugged her shoulders. "I guess things have changed."

Ferris looked preoccupied as she considered Diane's advice. Soon, she smiled, her mood buoyant. "So you said as long as I'm in love, it's cool, right?"

"That isn't what I said—"

Ferris bent down to gather several blueberries from a bush on the side of the path. "Oh!" she cried, pricking her thumb. As she drew her finger to her mouth, licking the trickle of blood, she said, "Heavy symbolism, huh?"

Diane laughed anxiously. "I've got the distinct feeling that I said the wrong thing."

"No, you didn't!" Ferris exclaimed. "Not at all." She could hardly wait to see Gary.

15

Painfully self-conscious, Ferris took off her shirt. No matter how hard she tugged, north or south, Cinder's string bikini didn't cover enough. Feeling utterly and absolutely brazen, she hid in the back row as Gary ran them through a series of calisthenic exercises by the pool. "Okay, here we go . . . Five, four, three—" The girls groaned loudly.

"Come on, ladies!" he called. "This'll warm you up."

"Is it good for the bust?" Penelope asked.

"It's good for the brain. Donkey kicks, let's go!" he commanded. "Everyone tone up their muscles." His muscles glistened in the sunlight.

Cinder pushed Ferris forward to the front row. She feared she was going to fall out of her suit with another kick, so she pulled at it again, acutely aware of Gary's presence.

"Quit doing that," Cinder whispered. "You look ridiculous."

"I feel ridiculous," she countered.

"Ferris doesn't need to tone up, does she?" Cinder asked Gary. "Isn't she in excellent shape?"

Ferris giggled with embarrassment. "Shut up, will ya!"

"Mr. Callahan," Sunshine added. "Doesn't Ferris have great legs?"

"And what a curve!" Carrots chimed in.

Gary nodded, smiling. "That's because she exercises diligently. Ladies, when you turn forty, you'll thank me. Now kick those legs. Higher! C'mon, a little bit higher!"

Suddenly Sunshine broke out of the line-up, ran to the side of the pool and returned with a plaid thermos. She winked at Cinder, who nodded conspiratorially.

"Uh, Mr. Callahan," she said, sidling up close to him. "We thought you might like this." She poured the golden liquid into a cup.

"What is it?" he asked, suprised amusement playing across the features of his face.

Sunshine chortled. "Ginseng."

"Thanks," he said, taking a sip. "Isn't that what some athletes drink?" He smiled.

"They're not the only ones," Sunshine said, giggling haplessly.

"Did you see that?" Cinder whispered in Ferris' ear. "He drank the potion. Now all you have to do is dive in—"

"I don't want to," Ferris admitted. "You know, I can't swim—"

"That's why," Cinder said, shoving her into the pool. "And make it look good!"

"Oh, God!" she screamed as she plummeted to the bottom. Her nose filled with water and she couldn't breathe. Desperately, her arms clawed for the rungs of an imaginary ladder, Gary's arms that would grasp her, someone or something. "Help!" she shouted, rising for a moment, then sinking again.

"Gary, she's drowning!" Cinder cried. "Ferris can't swim." All the girls rushed to the side of the pool.

He was already in the water, diving to the bottom.

"This is so romantic," Sunshine sighed, tears in her eyes. "He's going to save her life."

Gary grabbed the back of her bathing suit and dragged Ferris to the surface. She was coughing and sputtering water. He carried her out of the swimming pool, her arms around his neck. "She's all right!" he said, gently laying her down.

She was shivering but her eyes were open. She looked around, confused and shaken.

"Give her mouth-to-mouth resuscitation!" Carrots called.

"Yeah!" Chubby cried.

"She needs artificial respiration!" Cinder suggested.

"The kiss of life!" Sunshine added.

Gary unraveled Ferris' arms which were wrapped around his neck. "How do you feel?" he asked.

"Scared . . ." She covered her face with her hands.

Cinder strolled over to where they sat together. "She can't swim, Gary. Maybe you could teach Ferris . . ." Her voice was sugary.

"Sure," Gary replied, rumpling Ferris' hair. "You're fine . . ."

Cinder smiled triumphantly as she left the two of them alone. When, several minutes later, a lanky girl in a green tank suit headed toward the pool, she stopped her. "The pool's off limits until eleven o'clock."

"That's weird . . ." the girl said, walking away.

They stood together in the shallow end of the pool. Ferris' earlier close call had only increased her

fear of the water. But with Gary nearby, she moved slowly forward, until the water reached her shoulders. Then she drew back. "I can't," she said, kicking her legs but she still sank like a boulder. Gary pulled her up. She sputtered water and laughed simultaneously which made her choke.

"Keep your head up!" he said, grinning.

In the woods near the pool, Cinder and Sunshine spied on them, sharing one pair of binoculars, their heads bobbing with excitement. "Did you see that!" Sunshine cried.

"Play something," Cinder suggested, indicating her wooden recorder. "Hurry!"

Sunshine began playing a romantic ballad with a lilting, melancholy melody. Cinder watched as Gary tried to teach Ferris to float on her back. His arms were under her waist.

"Something sexy!" Cinder demanded. When Sunshine started playing an East Indian song that could have been an accompaniment to a belly dancer, Cinder applauded. "That's it!"

She picked up the binoculars again, watching as Ferris sunk underwater again. "This is getting a little boring," she commented wryly.

On the other side of the camp grounds, near the road, Angel and Dana were posted on top of a tree, gazing raptly through binoculars at some boys racing dirt bikes. Randy was among them, showing off as he tilted his bike all the way backwards so that he rode on one wheel. The dust flew around him like smoke.

"Wow!" Dana cried. "What a man!"

When his bike turned over and Randy ended up in a mound of dirt, he threw his helmet angrily.

Angel said, "He'll have to do, I guess." But her

sensuous smile revealed more. She peered through the binoculars intently.

Every afternoon that week, there was a swimming lesson for Ferris. As Sunshine played her sexy raga from a nearby perch, Gary placed his arms under Ferris' back as she attempted, once again, to float above the water.

"There," he said softly. "You see, there's nothing to be afraid of."

"Not with you around," she said, looking into his eyes as he bent over her. "I used to be so scared . . ."

His face was serious and thoughtful as he studied the young girl in his arms. Sometimes she seemed so much like a woman that he wanted to be with her, as a man. But at other times, as she giggled girlishly, her fifteen-year-old self radiated and he felt somewhat ridiculous. He slowly removed his arms, letting Ferris go.

"Oh!" she cried softly, beginning to sink. He caught her. She grasped his neck. He leaned away from her body.

In an effort to dispel the mood of intimacy between them, Gary said, "You're dead weight, Miss Whitney." Gently and not without some regret, he loosened her arms from around his neck.

She was disappointed. "You won't give up on me, will you?" Her eyes searched for affirmation in his.

He shook his head. "Nope."

She said, her voice almost a whisper, "You saved my life the other day." He smiled. "You did. Don't laugh." Her eyes were bright, her mouth seductive. "In China, if you save a person's life, you're responsible for them—forever." She hesitated, her voice dropping still lower. "Their souls marry or something, uh, like that . . ."

Gary cleared his throat loudly. "Hmmm. Right. Okay, if you say so." He shook his head. "Let's, uh, try getting you to float above water again, Miss Whitney."

She leaned back, dropping languidly into the water. His strong arms awaited her.

16

PARENTS' Day hit Camp Little Wolf like a howling typhoon. Bunks had to be tidied, dirty laundry hidden, skits performed and barbecue pits manned. Painted WELCOME PARENTS signs hung from all the cabin doors. Grown-ups lurked everywhere.

Some parents reacted to the sight of their darlings, tanned and healthy-looking, as if they hadn't seen them in years. Ear-wrecking screams greeted them as they clutched hankies, spilled tears and bickered good-humoredly. Hot dogs splattered with mustard and relish turned the camp grounds into a collage of yellow and green.

"So how're you doin' here?" Angel's mother asked as she stumbled in spiked heels on the uneven path. She wore a flimsy dress and her hair was stiff with hair spray.

Angel took her arm. "Watch out or you'll break your neck." She guided her past a volleyball game in progress.

Her mother studied the male counselors with interest.

"The kids are, uh, different here," Angel said.

"They read books and stuff." She carried a tray of franks and soda.

"Nobody's stopping you from reading . . . Not bad," she commented as she studied a young man in tennis whites.

"There's this girl here," Angel began, trying to get her attention. "And you know what she's doing? She and this counselor are writing the whole camp show."

"What'll that get her?" her mother asked, bored.

"What'll hot-wiring cars get me?"

She looked indulgently at her daughter. "Everybody's wild at your age. I was. God!" She rolled her eyes. "But you'll come out okay. You know what your problem is?" she said, turning to Angel. "You're a little jealous, that's all—and it's understandable. All these girls with their expensive clothes and—"

"I'm not talking about clothes!" Angel exclaimed, her face flushed with frustration. "I don't give a damn about that. It's something else . . ." She stared down at the ground. "They're not like me. Nobody else here punches, they—"

Her mother interrupted, putting her arm around Angel. "They're softies, that's why. You're a fighter. I'm proud of my little girl."

Angel turned to her, confusion and rage in her eyes. "Who am I fighting, Mom?"

They sat down together on a bench. Angel took an enormous bite into her hot dog. Her mother laughed, running her fingers through her daughter's dark hair. "That's my girl," she said.

"Can I ask you something?" Angel began unsurely.

"Sure." Her mother bit into her hot dog, raising her eyebrows.

"Personal. I mean, it's none of my business and all but I need to know . . ." Her voice quavered.

"I've got nothing to hide." They studied each other.

Angel paused, biting her lower lip. Then she blurted the words out. "When did you lose your virginity?"

Her mother's eyes grew large with surprise. "Oh, that."

"It's kind of important to me . . ." she explained.

"Let's see," her mother said. "I think I was nineteen." Her face revealed boredom and contempt. "Nineteen years old . . ."

"Nineteen!" Angel exclaimed, her voice dropping with disappointment. "That's ancient."

Her mother bit into her hot dog, patting her mouth with a napkin. "It was nothing then," she remarked indifferently. "It's still nothing." She straightened her dress over her knees.

Angel observed her. There was something so resigned and hurt about her. As if she didn't expect anything out of life besides a couple of tough breaks. It made her sad to see it.

"So why's everybody making such a big deal about it, huh?" Angel demanded.

Her mother shrugged her shoulders. "It's all romantic bullshit. Believe me, Angel, it's a crock." She crossed her legs as her eyes followed the archery counselor. "This place doesn't look so bad, not bad at all . . ." She tucked her bra strap under the shoulder of her dress. "Hmmmm . . ."

Angel saw it and shook her head. If it wasn't anything, how come her mother was always on the make?

Her mother reapplied her lipstick, peering at

the reflection in her sunglasses. "How do I look, honey?"

Angel wanted to flee from her, find Dana, Chubby, even Penelope. But instead she smiled wryly. "Terrific."

Strolling, her arm in her father's, Ferris passed the bench where Angel and her mother sat. They acknowledged each other by a nod of heads.

"Do you know her?" Angel's mother asked.

"Kind of."

"Her father looks loaded. She's a snob, right?"

"Oh, she's not that bad," Angel said, watching Ferris and her father as they walked to the lake together. She couldn't even imagine what it would be like to have a father you could hang out with, talking, sharing things. That was what Angel envied more than a bank account or anything else.

"Are her parents together?" her mother inquired pointedly.

"How am I supposed to know?"

"I bet they're split up," she said with some satisfaction.

A group of girls sporting FERRIS t-shirts jogged past. When they spotted their namesake, they cheered loudly. "Hey, Ferris!"

Mr. Whitney beamed with pride. "Looks like you've made some friends here, pumpkin," he said.

"Oh, Dad," she muttered.

Cabin A teemed with parents snooping around and asking questions. When Chubby's mother opened the drawer of her bureau and discovered fifty prophylactics, she gasped, quickly shutting the drawer.

"Is she getting any neater?" her father asked, his

chunky arm around his daughter. They shared a pint of vanilla ice cream, feeding each other.

"Oh, yes," her mother said, trying to compose her horror-filled face. "Much neater." Desperately, she turned to some of the other parents. Could it have been a hallucination? Her daughter didn't look any different.

"And what part are you going to play in the talent show?" she asked, sitting down next to her.

"You want some, Mom?" Chubby asked, passing her the spoon.

"My baby!" she cried, throwing her arms around her daughter.

Dana, Sunshine, Angel and Carrots gave their parents the guided tour, opening closet doors, showing hospital corners and neatly folded clothes. They displayed macrame wall hangings, ceramic ashtrays and Sunshine's stained glass window. Diane watched with amusement.

"This is so nice," Carrots' mother proclaimed happily. "Such fun you girls must have together." She folded her hands in her lap contentedly.

"Oh, yes," they chimed. "We have lots of fun."

Wearing a full-length poncho, Sunshine's father added, "Creativity is a primal force."

Cinder approached Dana's mother. "You have such an intelligent daughter. It's a pleasure to live with her. She's always reading . . ."

"That's our little bookworm," she crooned. "We're a book-loving family."

"Reads, reads, reads," Cinder continued, tossing a handful of books out of the drawer. "Can hardly get her outside . . ."

Dana hissed at Cinder. "Stuff it, okay?" She flung

herself on the floor, trying to hide the books with her body.

"And such interesting books . . ."

At that, the girls exploded in a fit of riotous giggles.

"Dana, stop it!" her mother cried, picking up a book from the floor. "What is this?" she asked. "Oh. *Sex Among Groups.*" She threw the book down in disgust. "Dana, come here. This minute! I want to talk to you."

"It's good," Sunshine's mother said. "They should be exposed to everything."

Staring at the bird feathers in her hair, Dana's mother shook her head in confusion. "Is that so?" she asked.

"Freedom is options."

"But how much freedom?" Chubby's mother demanded. She wrung her hands in an advanced state of shock.

"Are you all right, darling?" her husband asked.

She touched her forehead. "Of course I am, dear."

Angel and her mother sat on Ferris' bed, grinning. Angel showed her the rocks she'd collected while climbing with Diane.

The sun was setting behind the tall pines and the light breeze that had blown during the day was now turning chilly. Ferris shivered slightly as she watched the shafts of light slowly grow thinner until they were obscured by the shadows.

"Do you want to wear my jacket?" her father asked.

She shook her head, wrapping her arms around herself.

"Look," he said. "Maybe she'll come back. Your mother's an impulsive woman, Ferris."

"Where did she go?" she asked quietly.

He hesitated, closing his eyes. Then he said, almost in a whisper, "Reno."

She turned to look at him. "People get divorced in Reno . . ."

He nodded, staring helplessly around him.

"Why did you say she was coming back?" she demanded.

He dropped his arms at his side. "She said she might come back, that she just needed time to think—"

"In Reno?" Ferris demanded. "Oh, Dad . . ." She looked away from him, knowing that if their eyes met, she'd begin to cry and that wouldn't help anything. His eyes surrounded by dark circles revealed his own misery.

He nodded sadly. "You're probably right."

They walked across an old wooden bridge that creaked under their feet. "Do you think we'll make it?" he said, attempting a joke, but it had a sober ring of truth to it.

Ferris hastened her pace when they got to the other side as if she could outrace the fact that her mother had left them both. But it followed her like a chilling shadow.

He was out of breath, heaving loudly as he tried to keep up with his daughter. "Ho, you! Slow down! I'm out of shape." Ferris waited for him to catch up. "I have an idea!" he said brightly. "When you get back, maybe we'll take a trip up to Canada, rent a boat—" He tried to sound enthusiastic.

"Dad," Ferris began. "Would Mom have liked me better if I looked like her?" She pushed a strand of hair out of her face.

"I'm not even going to dignify that with an answer."

"I've—" She bit her lip, chewing on it desperately. "I've disappointed her. You can tell me. I've always known it anyhow."

He grabbed her arm angrily. "Your attitude's—"

"It's true!" Ferris screamed. "You know it is. Look at me, Dad!" she said, beginning to cry. "I'm not as pretty as—"

He interrupted her. "You're very attractive, Ferris."

"I don't fit in. I've never fit in," she wept unhappily.

"When your mother gets in touch with me, I'll make sure that she calls you. Okay?" he implored. "Everything's going to turn out for the best. I know it will."

"Why didn't she think of that herself?" Ferris demanded. "Since when do mothers have to be told to phone their kids?" She covered her face with her hands.

"Since they got liberated," he said wryly. "Look, she's re-evaluating her life, wondering if she wants to be a wife—"

"A mother—"

"She feels like she's never explored her own talents and possibilities," her father added, futility in his voice.

Ferris looked up at him, wiping her eyes. "She's scared of getting old and wrinkled, that's what it is. I'm not dumb. I know all about that change of life."

"Ferris," he said, "you don't—"

"We read about it in biology."

He smiled, shifting his weight from foot to foot uncomfortably. "I think there's more to it than that."

Ferris continued, trying to hide her feelings with a cavalier attitude. "I suppose you'll be going out with young girls soon," she said, scrutinizing him. "Twenty-year-olds . . ."

He turned guiltily away, not wanting to broach this subject with his daughter. When a mosquito landed on his neck, he slapped it ceremoniously. "Mosquitoes," he indicated.

"Dad," Ferris said, her voice vulnerable again.

"Yes?"

"You begged her to come home, didn't you? I mean, we shouldn't pretend to have pride now. Right?" Her eyes implored him.

He nodded sadly. "Believe me, I tried everything I could but she was determined to—"

"You sure it wasn't my fault?" She looked directly at him. "She used to get mad when my room was messy, when I wouldn't dress the way she wanted me to—"

He interrupted her abruptly. "It has nothing to do with you."

Ferris' expression was confused. "Sure, it does. She left me too . . ."

He sighed, shaking his head back and forth in ever widening arcs. "Do you need any money?" he asked, attempting a change of subject. "Do you have what you need? Those jeans of yours—"

"Mother hated the way I dressed," Ferris declared. "I guess I should have tried harder but—"

He chuckled at the irony of it all. "Ferris, she didn't leave because of your clothes."

She smiled foolishly, then she took her father's hands. "The truth, Dad. Are you dating now?"

He looked away, embarrassed. "I wouldn't exactly call it that. Ferris—"

She stared at him angrily, unaware that tears had started trickling from her eyes, down the sides of her nose. Her voice flattened to a dull monotone, as if keeping it that way, the feelings would be less devastating. It wouldn't be as if she had lost her mother—whom she had never really known or, more to the point, who had never known her. Her family wouldn't be together. She didn't want to believe it.

Finally Ferris said softly, "So it's over."

"What?" he asked, knowing the answer, trying to postpone the knowledge from himself and his young daughter.

"Nothing," she whispered inaudibly. "I'm sorry—"

"Ferris, don't—please."

She fell into his arms, crying inconsolably. "Dad, I want to die. I really do."

He stroked her hair gently, watching the last shafts of light flicker in the trees. There was already a pale wisp of a moon in the dusk sky. "It's for the best," he told her without conviction. "You'll see."

"No, it isn't!" She wept, beating her fists against his chest. "You always say that but it's not true. Nothing's for the best. Nothing!"

17

"HAPPY BIRTHDAY, CHUBBY!" The girls squealed as they carried a seven-layer mocha cream cake with chocolate icing. Sixteen candles glowed brightly. They set it before her.

"Oh! Wow! Whee!" she screamed hysterically. "Yummy!"

As Chubby was about to blow out the candles, Carrots commanded, "Make a wish."

"Okay," Chubby said. "I wish . . ." She ruminated aloud. "Uh—"

"Don't tell, silly," Sunshine interrupted. "Then it definitely won't come true."

Chubby squeezed her eyes shut, extinguishing all the candles in a hefty gust of breath. "There," she said proudly.

"Hooray!" they cheered. "Yay, Chubby! For she's a jolly good female . . ." they sang.

Chubby rubbed her hands together excitedly, hardly able to contain her anticipation to get into the good stuff, her cake. She took the biggest slice for herself, grinning sheepishly, "Well, it's my birthday!" Immediately, she began wolfing it down in enormous gulps. "This is great!" she exclaimed, her mouth full.

Sunshine looked disapproving. "That has a lot of sugar and you know what sugar does to you."

"What?" Dana asked, concern crossing her face.

"Depression," Sunshine said, closing her eyes ominously.

"You mean, it makes you fat," Cinder said, taking a sliver of cake which she picked at delicately.

Chubby ignored her, bringing a slice of cake to Ferris, who sat on her bed, staring despondently out the window.

"Ferris," she said softly.

She didn't respond, continuing to stare as if she hadn't even heard Chubby. Her eyes were vacant and her body limp.

"What's wrong with Ferris?" she asked the others.

Angel grabbed the slice and made it vanish in several generous bites. "Mmmm . . ." she smiled.

"Watch out!" Dana scolded. "Guys are turned off by porkiness."

Angel studied Dana's unseemly body and shook her head. "I appreciate the warning," she remarked sarcastically.

The following morning, Ferris lay in bed, her face turned to the wall. Around her, there was a hubbub of frantic activity. Some girls dressed, throwing sweat socks across the room, while others ripped open their mail. Dana sat on the floor, legs crossed, unwrapping a package. "What is this?" she asked impatiently. "It better be something good." She threw the brown paper on the floor.

"Maybe it's a care package," Carrots said hopefully, looking over her shoulder. "Candy, chocolate, potato chips—"

"Oh, no!" Dana cried. "They must be kidding!" She lifted a stack of six books. *"Little Women,"* she said contemptuously. *"The Scarlet Letter? Yuck! Tess of the D'Urbervilles*—I don't believe this!" She flung *Pride and Prejudice* at Carrots.

Cinder strutted over to Ferris' bed, shaking her. "Get up! You have a swimming lesson," she fumed. "Do you hear? Ferris!"

She didn't stir, pulling the blanket over her chin.

18

It was time to strike, Angel decided, that afternoon. She could see a group of boys swimming across the lake. Maybe Randy was there. She untied a camp canoe and started to paddle, a cigarette dangling from her mouth.

As soon as the boys caught sight of her, they began howling. Wolf whistles greeted her but Angel was undaunted. There was a look of determination on her face.

She spotted Randy as he was about to dive off the wharf. He squinted, shielding his eyes with his hand. Suddenly he recognized her and waved. She stopped paddling, allowing the canoe to float toward the shore.

"You! Beautiful!" one of the boys cried.

"Can I have a ride?" another screamed, swimming toward her boat. "C'mon . . ."

"Shove off," she said, her eyes on Randy. "Hey, you coming or not?" she called.

Embarrassed, he pointed to himself, looking around.

Angel patiently lit another cigarette.

The other boys patted Randy on the back. "She wants you," they said. "Hey, hey, hey!"

He felt unsure and a little intimidated, but he puffed out his chest and nodded to Angel. The boys whistled and slapped Randy's back again. He turned to them and cursed under his breath. Then he dived off the wharf and swam toward the canoe.

When he was within earshot, Angel said, "Get in, sucker."

As she paddled away from the shore, Randy watched her. "You're really something," he said, grinning.

"Here," Angel said, passing him a cigarette. She shot him a furtive smile. When he smiled back warmly, she frowned. "What are you looking at?"

He knitted his eyebrows in confusion.

Together, they secured the canoe under some brush on a secluded part of the shore. Then they began walking. As far as they could see, it was trees and more trees. They were the only ones for miles. It was like being the first man and woman. Angel wanted to kick herself for having such a corny thought. The sun, in the middle of the sky, cast brilliant rays of light. Both puffed on cigarettes.

"Do you want to stop?" Randy asked.

She shrugged. "I don't care."

They sat down next to each other. "How's Little Wolf?" Randy asked, picking up a blade of grass which he twisted.

She ignored his question. "Beer?"

He was startled. "Sure."

She took two cans out of her knapsack. With cool expertise, she popped both of them open, handing him one.

"Thanks." He hesitated, then grinned slightly.

She toasted him absently. "Cheers."

"Where'd you get these?" he asked.

Angel glanced at him. "I brought them from home."

He toasted her approvingly. "Good thinking, Angel."

"Don't let the name fool you," she told him.

He laughed loudly. The sound reverberated off of the trees. Then he looked around uncomfortably. "All this nature stuff's for the birds, you know what I mean?"

Angel nodded. "It's the pits."

But both watched the way the sun's rays moved over the trees, hitting a cluster of leaves so that they momentarily glowed, then another one. For a while the light played on their faces. Randy closed his eyes languidly. Was she boring him?

Angel lit another cigarette, her eyes alert and calculating. "Have another beer?" she suggested.

He opened his eyes, leaning on his elbow to face her. "What's the rush? I haven't finished my first beer."

"Oh," Angel said. "Well, why don't you hold on to this one, so when you're ready and all? . . ."

He studied her, his mouth forming a half-smile. "You making out all right at Little Wolf?"

She grunted. "I'll live."

He relaxed, propping his back up against the trunk of an oak tree, then patted the ground next to him, indicating that Angel should move closer.

Her eyes narrowed as she watched the trees sway in the light afternoon breeze. Then she brightened. "Are you ready for your next beer?"

"Okay," he nodded amiably. "Chug-a-lug, huh?"

She smiled, banging her can into his. "Chug-a-lug."

He winked at her. Angel had to admit that he

sure was sexy. His dark eyes and muscular adolescent body held the promise of all sorts of new delights for her. She wanted to be close to him, to have his strong arms around her. Why did she hold back, she wondered. What was there to be afraid of? But something made her sit several feet from him, sipping her beer and smoking cigarettes as if her lungs were on fire and only more smokes would help. He did not look fearsome. In fact, everything about him from his easy smile to the tight cut of his jeans invited her, made her want to be close to him.

He drank his second beer contentedly. Not many girls would paddle across a lake to see you and come prepared with booze and smokes. But Angel was unique, tough talking and acting, a cigarette always hanging from her mouth. Nevertheless, he detected a softness about her that she kept secret, as though if somebody found out, the world would blow up. Maybe it was her world that she feared would explode if someone entered and got too close.

"This is nice," he muttered.

"You really have a way with words," she retorted.

"What's wrong with what I said?" he demanded. "How come you make me feel as if everything I say is stupid?"

"I'm sorry," she apologized. "Hey, chug-a-lug!" she said, toasting him again.

He smiled. "If I didn't know any better, I'd think you were trying to get me drunk."

"Maybe I am," she added, her eyes twinkling.

"O-kay!" he exclaimed, guzzling the rest of his beer down in one swallow.

"Wow-whee!" Angel teased.

He belched, grabbing his chest.

Angel poised her beer over her mouth and chugged down the rest. "A pro," he remarked.

She grinned with pride.

Both were beginning to feel a warm glow that was only partly inspired by the alcohol. Angel leaned back against a tree stump. She picked a dandelion and blew the feather petals at him. He tried to catch them in his fingers. The breeze scattered them.

"You got any more of those beers in your knapsack?" he inquired, smiling slyly.

"Sure," she said, popping open two cans.

An hour and four beers apiece later, Randy lay on the ground. Angel's expression was of pure and unmitigated disgust. She bent over him.

"You were supposed to get turned on, stupid!" she complained. "Not pass out! Jesus, a corpse on my hands!"

19

DIANE stood by Ferris' bed, gently touching her arm. Cinder and Sunshine watched over her shoulder.

"I can't help you if you don't tell me what's wrong," she implored. "Ferris—" Her voice was full of concern.

"She's been like that all morning," Sunshine said.

"Damn it," Cinder muttered, stamping her foot angrily.

Ferris continued to stare at the wall, her expression frozen. If she held herself that way, she imagined, maybe she wouldn't feel any of it. The pain inside her threatened to burst. It frightened her. She kept her mind blank, squeezing her eyes shut, not thinking about *anything*. But flashes intruded, no matter how hard she tried to stop them. How her father had looked, suddenly so old and vulnerable, as if it were a struggle for him not to break down and weep. She couldn't bear it. And her mother, so beautiful, a stranger now. Would she ever see her again? And what of the family? It no longer existed. They would never have Christmas or birthdays together. But there had been so many times when they had all been in different spots on the globe. Ferris did not think about any of these things. The blankness of the wall comforted her.

Diane turned to the girls, worried. "When did this start?"

Carrots joined them, adding her two cents' worth. "She didn't even have a piece of Chubby's cake last night—"

"Isn't that amazing," Cinder said sarcastically. Her eyes shone with malice. "I bet it has something to do with Parents' Day . . ." She paused dramatically. "And the fact that Ferris' father came—and her mother didn't."

At the sound of her words, Ferris' body quivered helplessly. But she did not stir from facing the wall.

"Yeah, she seemed upset after that," Sunshine added.

"Damn it," Cinder repeated under her breath, turning to Sunshine and Carrots. "Now what are we going to do?"

Diane watched this exchange curiously and then told the girls, "She can stay in this morning, but Ferris has to be at activities this afternoon."

At that, Ferris drew the blankets above her chin.

The sun blazed across the archery range, forcing the girls to shield their eyes in order to see the targets. Gary stood behind Carrots, showing her how to pull the bow. She giggled nervously as Gary drew her arm away from the bow.

"There now," he coaxed her. "Let it go slowly but steadily. And keep your eyes on the target. Easy does it . . ."

"I can't!" Carrots squealed, jumping from foot to foot.

"There's nothing to be afraid of. Just draw your

arm back, then let it go slowly." He released Carrots' arm but it jerked forward, sending an arrow that missed the whole target by several feet. Her face turned a tomato shade of red.

"You see what I mean?" she cried.

"One more time," he said, cocking another arrow in the bow. "But this time, eyes on the target . . ."

"Do I have to?" she groaned. She secretly enjoyed the attention, yet the physical contact made her anxious.

As he helped her draw the bow back, he saw Ferris walking slowly to the archery range. "Just a minute," he told Carrots, studying her. Ferris looked like she was sleep-walking, her body listless, her face dazed. Her hair was uncombed and her clothes slept-in. None of the vivacity and charm which attracted him to her was in evidence. It worried him.

But he turned his attention back to Carrots. "Are we ready?" he asked. "You too." He turned to the others.

Cinder whispered in his ear, "Ferris needs you."

Carrots heard it and added, "She sure does."

He chuckled, aware that the girls were trying to get him interested in Ferris. "I'll get to her," he said. "Right now, you need me," he told Carrots. "Let's see you shoot a bullseye.

"Pull that bow back," he continued. "Come on, Carrots. Farther! Farther! Let's use those muscles! Everybody, take aim—"

"I don't have any," Carrots complained but pulled the bow back anyway. Sunshine and Cinder did too.

"My parents don't want me to get into competitive sports," Sunshine remarked, her bow cocked.

"Imbecile," Cinder said. "Archery's not competitive."

Gary continued down the line. "Sunshine, you have to hold the bow steady." He straightened her arm.

"I'm trying," she said.

Dana pulled Cinder aside. "How are we supposed to know when 'it' happens?"

Cinder's attention was on Ferris. She turned to face Dana. "What are you talking about?"

Dana grew embarrassed. "What I mean is, do we have to watch when they—you know . . ."

Cinder's tone was disdainful. "You sound a little inexperienced, dear."

Dana blanched momentarily, looking around herself from Sunshine to Carrots. "It's not that, but I was just wondering—"

Sunshine improvised. "Uh, when I became a woman, my eyes tilted . . ." She smiled, wrinkling her nose. Then she turned to Cinder for approval.

Cinder nodded suspiciously.

"Oh, yeah! Right!" Dana exclaimed. "I remember. And their faces get all shiny and a look of contentment is in their eyes. Sure. No problem."

Cinder shrugged. "Sometimes I wonder about some of you, whether you know anything or are just bulling—"

"Not me," Dana said, shaking her head.

"Ditto," Sunshine added.

Carrots, who caught the last part of the conversation, rushed to join in. "Double ditto for me."

Ferris picked up her bow, staring absently at the target. Then she dropped it and started to walk away as if she'd forgotten why she had even come. Cinder picked up her bow angrily. She was about to say something but Ferris wandered past her.

Gary was helping Chubby, who protested, "I don't want to be skinny! Why won't anyone believe me? I want to be voluptuous and ripe like a melon."

Her face was sweaty from the hot sun and the effort of holding back the string of her bow.

Gary laughed. "Okay, now. Even if you don't want to be skinny, some muscle tone wouldn't kill any of you."

Ferris wandered past them, not even noticing Gary. He told Chubby, "Excuse me a minute." Then he caught up with Ferris. "Hey, I waited for you at the pool," he said.

She stared past him, her voice a controlled monotone. "I forgot."

He walked several steps with her, trying to draw her out. "Has anything happened?"

"No."

"Ferris," he implored, putting his arm around her shoulder. "Something seems very wrong . . ."

The gentleness in his voice threatened to break through like a thin shaft of light on a dark, murky lake. She knew he would understand, that they could talk, he was her friend. But she couldn't do it. She looked away from him.

"Okay," Gary said. "When you feel like talking, I'm here. I want you to remember that."

He ran back to Chubby, whose eyes were narrowed, concentrating on the target. "I think I can do it," she said, pulling back the bowstring.

"Hold it," Gary called. "You're looking terrific!"

Chubby released the arrow which went straight into the red center of the target.

Everyone cheered her.

"One more time," Gary said, passing her another arrow.

"Do I have to?" she asked. Chubby drew the string back as far it would go, then let the arrow go. It hit a nearby tree.

Cinder dropped her bow angrily and ran up to

Ferris. She looked tall and imposing. Ferris just stared at her.

"I have no intentions of losing, damn you!" she screamed. "Angel's going to get to fourth base to-night. Do you hear me?"

Ferris turned away. Cinder grabbed her roughly. "Look, bitch, get yourself together. I don't give a damn what's bugging you. You have something to do—"

Ferris tried to free herself from Cinder's hold. There were four white marks on her arm.

"Nobody makes a fool of me. Is that clear!" Cinder cried, walking away in a furious huff.

20

SOME of the girls were in pajamas already, passing around cream-filled cookies. Carrots and Sunshine sat on the floor, hunched over a backgammon board. Carrots wore red and white striped pajamas with red felt feet. Cinder stopped in front of them. "Ex-c-u-u-u-se me," she said contemptuously, climbing over them. Sunshine stared at her red satin nightie.

"Girls!" Diane called, closing the screen door behind her. "Has anyone seen Ferris?"

"Nope."

"I didn't either."

"She was at dinner," Chubby said.

"No, she wasn't," Dana interrupted, glancing up from her paperback, *Fear of Flying*.

Diane looked around anxiously. "If anyone sees her, will you please let me know? I'll check the grounds."

Angel stood in front of the mirror, mounds of makeup stacked in front of her. They were "contributions" from Dana, Chubby, even Penelope. She applied lipstick gingerly, as if it might be her first time.

As she was about to put the finishing touches on her upper lip, Cinder bumped into her accidentally on purpose. "Oh, I'm so sorry," she said.

Angel made a fist and was about to slug her, when she stopped herself. She wiped off the smudged lipstick, then began to sing, "Tonight's the night . . ."

"You better pray," Cinder said, slinking away. "I don't know who'd want you."

"We'll see about that," Angel sneered. "By the way, what happened to Ferris?"

"You tell me," she answered angrily.

All evening, Ferris had walked, hoping if she kept in motion, the thoughts could not catch up to her. She had gone past the camp grounds on to the road where she wandered for several hours. But as the sky grew darker, she started walking back.

She could see the lights in all the cabins. It looked warm inside. How she longed to be in her bed, the covers over her. There was a chill in the air and she was only wearing a thin t-shirt and cut-offs. But the thought of seeing the other girls, with their questions and intrusive looks, made her turn in the opposite direction. She walked to the lake.

The moon was still faint but the inky water caught its reflection. She stepped into an empty rowboat, wrapping her arms around herself. A soft, steady sound issued from the boat. Ferris was crying.

Angel had difficulty stuffing herself into a pair of tight blue jeans, but finally she pulled the zipper up. Penelope sprayed her with Rive Gauche as Dana paced up and down nervously, coaching Angel. Chubby tried to fix her hair but Angel pushed her away.

"Now remember," Dana said, "don't be scared.

There's nothing to be scared about. That's the most important thing. Just don't be worried . . ." She clenched her teeth anxiously.

"Will all of you stop breathing down my neck," Angel exclaimed. "You'll make my eyeballs steam up."

"And don't, Angel, under any circumstances, talk about your past," Dana continued. "That turns men off."

Angel grinned at her. "Idiot, I don't have a past, remember?"

"I mean, don't get personal with him and ask a lot of questions . . ." Dana added.

"Why not?" she demanded.

Dana looked confused. "I don't know. I've always heard that, though."

Penelope turned sagely to the both of them, "Men are afraid of falling in love."

"What do you know?" Angel asked, but was struck by the wisdom of Penelope's words. She stared at her momentarily.

"Just try your best," Dana said, trying another tack. "And remember, we'll all be there with you."

"Oh, yeah?"

"Figuratively," Dana added. "In spirit if not in the flesh. And remember what Shakespeare said, 'Lilies that fester smell far worse than weeds.'" She smiled proudly.

"Huh?"

Dana shook Angel's hand, nodding with determination. "You'll do fine. I'm sure of that." Angel's expression revealed her uncertainty. "Good luck."

"It can't be all that bad," Chubby added. "If it were, everybody wouldn't be doing it and there wouldn't be all those movies and books . . ."

"Okay, already . . ." Angel lifted the collar of her

denim jacket. "And don't wait up for me, fellas." She smiled confidently but as soon as she was out the door, she realized her legs were weak and her stomach queasy.

Ferris had taken the boat out to the middle of the lake. But now as she tried to row back, the boat spun in circles. She looked down at the water which had been calm earlier. It was choppy, rocking the little rowboat from side to side. Ferris held on to both sides, trying to steady the boat. Once she had tried to call out for help. Her voice echoed back to her, and then it was silent.

All the "if onlys" came rushing to her. If only she had not taken the boat out, but instead had returned to cabin A. If only she had continued her swimming lessons with Gary, so that she could swim back to safety. If only he were there to save her. If only she hadn't been such a damn fool. She tried to row again, exerting equal pressure on both oars. The boat began its 360 degree circle one more time.

Angel thought she heard a cry for help and stopped paddling. She listened intently but it was not repeated. Nerves, she told herself, as she reached the other side of the lake. Looking behind her, all that she could see was darkness. The stars were obscured by menacing rain clouds.

She stuck two fingers between her lips and gave a wolf whistle that pierced the night. Ferris heard it or, at least, she thought she did. She stared at the other side of the lake.

Randy heard it too as he slept in a tent with two other boys. He leaped into his jeans and sweatshirt, running his hand over his hair.

When he ran out of the tent, he spotted Angel in

her canoe, paddling to the shore. He grinned with admiration.

"What if they catch you?" he called.

She shrugged. "I'll tell them I'm an insomniac."

He laughed.

"Are you coming or what?"

Randy ran to meet Angel's canoe. "Get in, sucker," she teased, lighting two cigarettes.

The water pushed Ferris' boat farther and farther away from the camp grounds. Although she continued to row, her efforts were futile. When thunder sounded, she crawled into the bottom of the boat. Her teeth chattered. She grasped the oars, hearing the water slapping against the side of the boat.

21

THE rain had started as a light sprinkle, spitting droplets on them in intervals of several seconds. Now it was really coming down. Angel looked up angrily at the sky. "What now?" she asked.

"I know a place we can go," Randy offered.

"Where?"

"The boat house."

"You show me where it is."

As Randy directed, Angel paddled the canoe toward the nearby shore. After they tied the boat to a wooden log that projected into the water, they scrambled up the bank into the tiny shelter.

There were several missing planks on the floor. Randy took her hand to help. Angel drew it away. The roof was broken and the rain dripped in. She stared around herself.

"Hey, Angel!" he called. "Come over here. It's dry." Randy stood on the other side, leaning against the wall.

She walked over to him shyly, lighting a cigarette. He drew a smoke from the pack in his t-shirt sleeve.

"Are you going with anybody?" Angel asked.

"No," he answered, smiling. "There's a girl—she works at the candy counter. But we're not, uh . . . You know?"

Angel moved closer to him. "You're not fooled by my name, are you, Randy?" She grinned, her expression seductive.

He put his arm around her. She wrapped her arms around his waist. As they began to kiss, she felt herself yielding to the softness of his lips, to the way he held her so tight.

All of a sudden, her eyes popped open. His were still closed, continuing to kiss her. She glanced around nervously. He unbuttoned the first button on her shirt, then the second one.

"Don't!" she cried, pulling away from him.

Surprised, he asked, "What's wrong?"

"Nothin' . . ." She looked away from him toward the door as if she wished she could flee. Then she turned back to him. "Okay," she said, gritting her teeth.

She pulled a small, folded brown paper bag out of her jeans and tossed it to him. Her manner was brisk and businesslike, a desperate attempt to hide her intense fear and nervousness.

He looked at the bag without opening it. "What is it?" he asked, his eyes imploring hers. She buttoned her shirt.

"Well, open it," she sneered. "It's so I don't get pregnant, stupid." Angel kicked a twig near her foot.

He shook his head, startled. "How come you're not on the pill?" he mumbled self-consciously.

"I'm allergic to it," she said. "Turn around."

"What?" he asked, shaking his head with exasperated confusion. "I don't get it."

"Turn around," she repeated angrily. "I have to take my clothes off, don't I?"

He stepped toward her, dropping his voice to a romantic whisper. "I'll help you."

She sent him a dirty look. He stopped, bewildered.

"I don't need any help," she insisted, then stomped over to a dark corner of the boat house. Her fingers were shaking so badly she had difficulty unbuttoning her shirt.

Randy followed her, his head cocked to the side as he watched. She turned on him. "Are you going to just stand there or what?"

"Angel—" he began, his arms dangling at his sides.

"I thought you were going to get undressed."

"Yeah, sure . . ."

"Well?" She glared at him.

"What?"

"Go ahead," Angel urged, turning her back to him.

He looked dumbfoundedly at her but began to slip off his t-shirt. "Not here!" she demanded, pointing to the opposite side of the boat house. "Over there."

He smiled, trying to please her. As he walked away, he tossed his shirt in the air. "You're kinky," he remarked.

"And don't forget the . . . stuff in the package," Angel called.

He began to pile up some straw, patting it so it made a cozy pallet for them. "It'll be warm here," he said, sitting down.

"Big deal," she muttered, standing in the corner, cold, frightened, wishing that she could run, and yet—he was being so nice. She wanted to slug herself for being such a chickenshit. Her hands trembled as she struggled with another button. "Damn!" she cursed under her breath, impatient with herself.

She could see Randy sitting there. His back looked like a young boy's, but it was strong and muscular. "Pipe down," she told herself, taking a deep breath. Finally she grabbed a cigarette from the pack and lit up.

"Hey, you getting high?" Randy called. "Good idea."

He stood up, walking toward her.

"Stay there!" she cried.

"Is that grass?" he asked, sniffing the air.

"No," she admitted.

As she continued to smoke, taking long puffs and exhaling slow, perfect rings, he started to pace up and down.

"You going to smoke the whole thing?" he asked impatiently.

"Why not?" she asked. "Smoking relaxes me."

"I'm getting undressed," he said finally, turning away from her. "I don't believe any of this," he muttered.

Out of the corner of her eye, Angel watched as he took off his jeans. He removed everything but his white B.V.D.s. Angel thought how white his skin was, so young. She still stood in all her clothes, finishing her cigarette.

He turned to her angrily, "What is this, a twenty-four-hour smoke or what?"

She felt even more insecure, almost choking on her cigarette. "Shut up!" she screamed.

"You'll stink of tobacco."

"Hold your nose!"

"You going to stay there all night?" he asked, looking down at his own body. He was beginning to feel more and more foolish as he waited for her to undress. But he called, "The bed's ready . . ."

"Straw," she said contemptuously.

"Angel," he implored.

"Stop nagging me!"

"I'm freezing my ass off . . ."

She darted forward, listening intently. "Is the rain coming in there? I don't want to do it where there's rain."

"It's dry," he said, his spirit dropping as he got colder and madder.

"You sure?"

He muttered softly to himself, "Oh, shit. Man, a weirdo." Then he called to her, "Yeah! Positive! C'mon!"

"Okay," she said. "But turn around."

"I'm way over here, Angel. We going to fool around all night or what?" His voice revealed his impatience which was making his mood nasty.

"Don't yell at me!" she cried.

Angel sat down and began to unlace her sneakers, still puffing on her cigarette. "If you forget to put that 'thing' on, I'll kill you. I'm not getting myself pregnant."

As she yanked at a button of her shirt, it came off, rolling to the floor. She got on her knees to search for it continuing to babble nervously. "I'm just not ready or willing to take care of some guy's brat, not yet. I don't know what's with men . . . They never come prepared. They think it's the woman's responsibility nowadays."

"You ready?" he asked hopelessly.

"Don't rush me!"

He darted to his feet, grabbing his jeans. "You can take all night, for all I care," he said finally. "I wouldn't touch you if you paid me!"

She turned to him. "What the hell's wrong with you?"

He slipped into his jeans. "I ain't interested, that's what."

She approached him, her feelings hurt. "Why?"

"Because you talk too much." He reached for his shirt.

"What are you mad at?" she asked fearfully.

"Who's mad?" He sat down to put on his shoes. "I'm not turned on by you, that's all. You're not my type."

When he was finished, Angel looked like she had been punched in the face. He continued to lash out at her, feeling humiliated and taunted. "I'm into older women. Kids your age don't—"

"I'm as old as you are," she interrupted. "You're in love with her, huh? You and that candy-counter chick." She wanted him to contradict her, to say it wasn't so.

"She knows how to act around a man!"

Angel backed away slowly as if each word of his entered her, hurting.

"You're a tease, that's what you are. I'm onto your game. A big talker! You lead the guy on but when it comes to doing it—"

"I was getting ready," she said faintly.

"Yeah? Well, too bad. Go find yourself someone else. I'm not wasting my time on you." He walked away from her, to the door of the boat house.

"I'm not sexy to you?" she asked very softly.

"All girls are sexy to me," he answered.

"Come on," she pleaded. "You can take my shirt off if you want to . . ." She chewed on her bottom lip miserably. "Randy—"

"Some other time," he said. "Let's go."

Angel felt the tears forming around her eyes, inside of her nose. "But I like you."

"I don't care!" he cried, frustrated. "Let's get the hell out of here."

He walked ahead of her to the boat. She followed slowly behind him, her hands shoved in her pockets. The rain spilled on them, turning the ground into mud. Their feet sank in.

"Randy!" Angel called, running to catch up with him.

He untied the canoe. "You comin'?"

She climbed into the boat, grabbing the paddles. He sat down on the other side, pushing off from the log.

As she began to paddle, Angel stared at him, searching for some warmth on his face, like he still liked her. There was none.

He ran his fingers like a comb through his soaked hair.

"Maybe tomorrow?" Angel asked.

He didn't answer.

"Randy, do you hear me?" she demanded, hurt written all over her face.

"Yeah," he answered, refusing to meet her eyes.

"Okay?"

"I don't know," he muttered.

As she paddled, they sat silently across from each other. Several times, she smiled tentatively at him, hoping that he might grin or something. But he stared stonily ahead at Camp Tomahawk's green night light on the pier.

Randy climbed out of the boat as soon as they reached the shore. He was about to walk away. Angel didn't know if she'd ever see him again. If she had blown it for good.

"Do you think—" she began, biting her lip desperately. "That we, uh, can see each other again?"

He looked at her unhappily. "Sure."

"Really?" she asked, her eyes brightening.

He nodded.

As she started rowing away from the shore, he watched for a moment. Then he ran back to his tent.

22

THE little rowboat threatened to capsize. Ferris struggled, shifting her weight to the upraised side. The water was dark and turbulent as was the rain above her. It was getting worse.

Grabbing the oars, she started rowing desperately. The boat rocked back and forth precariously. She grasped the sides, trying to hold on. One of the oars slipped out of her hands. Ferris leaned over, attempting to reach it.

Far more experienced, Angel managed to paddle her canoe across the lake. But her face was tense. She looked up at the sky, raising her voice angrily, "Turn it off!"

It was as if the outside elements reflected what was going on inside of her. Why had she been such a fool with Randy? What had made her so frightened? It wasn't a big deal, right? And then Randy had gotten pissed off with her. Was it really over between them? Her own stupidity and cowardice triumphed once again. And all these waterworks didn't help one bit. "Did you hear me!" she yelled at the storm clouds.

Ferris was halfway out of her boat, trying to capture the oar. Suddenly the boat tilted. She was flung into the water, screaming, her arms flapping to reach the boat.

"Help!" she cried, feeling the water pull her down. "HELP! HELP! HELP!" She gasped and disappeared underwater.

For a moment, Ferris rose out of the water, her arms reaching for some invisible savior. She coughed as if she were choking. "Somebody help me!" she cried. "Somebody!"

Then she disappeared again.

Angel heard it. Her eyes sharpened, trying to penetrate the night. "Where are you?" she called.

When there was no answer, she began paddling hastily, yelling, "Where are you? Tell me! How am I supposed to help you?" She peered into the darkness.

Then she saw her. Ferris' hair covered her face and her body was limp. "Stay there!" Angel called, diving into the water. Ferris sank below the surface again.

Angel's arms cut through the water as she plunged. She swam underwater until she reached Ferris, pushing her to the surface, trying to gasp for air herself. When she slipped under again, Angel darted below. For several seconds, there wasn't a sign of either of the girls. The rain and wind beat against the canoe and rowboat.

The sound of thunder was followed by a flash of lightning on the water. Angel resurfaced, holding Ferris by the collar of her shirt. She was thrashing and choking. Angel tried to regulate her own breathing. Ferris' eyes were panic-stricken.

"Cut it out!" Angel screamed. "Goddammit, hold still!" She struggled to hold on to Ferris, trying to swim back to the rowboat. The waves made it bob farther and farther away.

"Float," Angel commanded. "I'll drag you over there." When Ferris began to sink again, she said, "Float. Do you hear me?" She grasped at her shirt.

"I can't," Ferris whispered faintly.

"Yes, you can!" Angel screamed. "Come on, bitch!"

Ferris tried to turn over onto her back. She flapped her arms at her side and kicked her legs. Still, she began to submerge. "Nothing happens," she said.

Angel smacked her furiously across the face. "Float, damn it! What am I going to do with you?" she cried, looking around herself desperately.

Ferris' body stiffened at Angel's words. Thus she managed to remain above the water for several seconds. Angel pulled her by the hair and started towing her toward the rowboat, muttering, "Stupid bitch."

Angel was growing tired. She could see the boat but it was still a distance from them. She was chilled, her arms stiff and aching. But she continued pulling Ferris, complaining bitterly, "I have to do everything around here . . ."

When they finally reached the boat, both held on to the sides. Angel's breathing was heavy. Ferris wept.

"Shut the hell up!" Angel said, climbing into the boat. As she sat down, her face revealed her exhaustion and tension. She turned to look disgustedly at Ferris, who clung to the side of the boat.

"Well, are you going to come in or what?" she

demanded, grabbing Ferris' hand. With some difficulty, she hauled her into the boat.

Ferris was trembling violently. Her skin had turned to a pale shade of blue. The rain continued to beat down on them.

Angel started paddling with one oar as fast as she could. Ferris' hands covered her face as she kept on crying.

"Did you hear me! I said, shut up!" Angel screamed.

Ferris bit her lip, but it still quivered nonstop. Her eyes were puffy, her skin covered with goose bumps. When she began to cough, clutching her chest with her hand, Angel said, "If you puke on me, I'll dump you. I swear." She was paddling rapidly, turning to look at Ferris every few moments, worried.

"I'm starting to feel like a chauffeur. Stop shaking, will you! You're making me nervous." She glared at Ferris. "I should be the one crying, dummy."

Ferris nodded weakly, willing to agree with anything.

Angel groaned loudly. "Asshole," she cried. "What the hell are you doing on the lake? You can't swim."

"I was thinking," she answered miserably.

"Think on the john like everybody else," Angel retorted.

"My mom's run off," she began, looking to Angel in the hope of understanding and support.

"So," she said. "Mine splits a couple times a year."

"She does?" Ferris asked, amazed.

Angel mimed her nastily, annoyed by her vulnerability yet touched by it. "Yeah, 'she does.' "

"Does she come back?" she asked hopefully.

Angel shrugged. "Sure. Well, sort of. When she finds a guy, they usually send for me."

"Oh."

Fury rushed out of her at Ferris. She did not know why but she cried, "You've had your mother for fourteen years. That's forever. And you're making such a big deal about it. You're such a pain! I can't believe it!" She shook her head contemptuously. "Look around. Half the kids at camp have two fathers and one mother or one mother and no father —or nobody at all!" She laughed bitterly.

Ferris took a soggy embroidered handkerchief out of her pocket. She blew her nose.

"Angel," she said, looking at her. "Thank you very much for saving my life."

Angel was astounded, watching her with her pathetic wet hanky trying to blow her nose. And now this, said so formally. She felt truly sorry for her. Ferris looked miserable. But she refused to show it.

"I didn't know it was you," Angel declared. "Believe me, if I did and had known what a pain you'd turn out to be, I'd have let you drown."

Ferris smiled slightly. "No, you wouldn't."

Angel's eyes darkened. "Don't bug me, Ferris."

23

A MOUNTAIN of washed dishes faced Angel, who had dropped her dish towel momentarily to mop her forehead with her sleeve. Ferris stood over the sink, dipping plates with meat gravy and mashed potatoes into the soapy water. The steam rose in hot clouds. Both looked grimy and exhausted.

Cinder peeked into the kitchen, her hair just washed and set so that it was a mass of shiny curls. "Hi, girls!" she called, waving. "Too bad you can't join us."

Angel ignored her. Ferris, who scrubbed a burnt pot with steel wire, glared at Cinder.

"Ta ta!" she said.

"I wish to hell this summer would end," Angel muttered after she left. "This is the pits."

"Me too," Ferris said, making a face.

"Will you stop being so damned agreeable," Angel complained.

"I'm sorry."

"That's exactly what I'm talking about," she sneered. "And I wish you wouldn't go blabbering around about how I hauled you out of the lake to everybody—"

"Okay, I'll try," Ferris said well-meaningly, passing her a plate.

Angel grabbed it from her. "Look, we're stuck on K.P. together and that's it. After this is over, don't say another word to me. And believe me, if I thought all this crap would happen, I would've left you in the lake." She frowned, her dark eyes covered by her long lashes.

"If that's the way you feel about it," Ferris began. "I—"

Angel moaned as she fetched several forks from a pile of flatware, drying them simultaneously. "Shut up, already . . ."

Their first evening of freedom was a camp fire. A clear night, the stars sparkled everywhere in the dark sky. There were hamburger patties, franks and marshmallows on a table. The girls stuck them on sticks which they held in the fire. Chubby was on her fifth burger.

Ferris stood there, roasting a hot dog. She watched Gary playing the guitar on the other side of the fire, his voice rich and melodic.

"Five hundred miles, five hundred miles . . . ," he crooned as the other counselors and some of the girls sang with him.

She smiled shyly at him, dropping her hot dog into the fire. "Oh, shoot!" she cried.

Cinder walked past her, saying spitefully, "You can't do anything right, can you?"

"I don't know what you mean," Ferris answered.

"Yes, you do," she sneered, nodding toward Gary. Sunshine looked at her sympathetically but followed Cinder. When Ferris tried to join them, she was met by stony glances.

Angel sat with her "team," who were cheering boisterously. Dana moseyed over next to her. "So when will he be able to see you?" she inquired.

"Not for a couple days," Angel muttered. "They caught him out after curfew . . ."

"Maybe you should get another boy," Chubby suggested.

Angel took a large bite out of her hot dog.

"What's with her?" Dana asked, pointing to Ferris who stood watching the fire, another hot dog on her stick.

"Is she still going to do it with Gary?" Chubby asked.

"How am I supposed to know?" Angel grumbled.

Sunshine touched Cinder's arm. "You know, I've been thinking," she began. "Losing your virginity should be a private thing . . ."

Cinder turned to her suspiciously. "Are you positive you still aren't 'intacto'?" she demanded.

Sunshine shook her head. "This is bad karma."

"All right," Cinder said, standing up. "Go ahead. Quit. We'll just turn our money over to Angel's team."

"What I meant is . . ." Sunshine muttered. "It just doesn't seem cool anymore."

"Suit yourself," Cinder remarked. "But you don't have your residual check riding on it."

She strutted over to where Ferris stood, staring dreamily into the fire as she listened to Gary's voice. Several times their eyes had met. He smiled at her warmly. Ferris looked down, knowing that he was watching her and that she was flirting with him.

"You know," Cinder said, dropping her voice to

a conspiratorial whisper, "you really let all of us down."

Ferris' expression was impassive. "I'm going to him tonight," she said quietly.

Sunshine and Carrots had joined them. Both were shocked.

"Really!"

"You're kidding!"

Cinder smiled knowingly. "I'll lend you my negligee."

Ferris looked at him firmly. "I don't think I'll need it."

Sunshine and Carrots began giggling. Soon they were falling all over each other in hysteria.

24

FERRIS lifted the hem of her white nightgown as she sneaked across the camp grounds to where Gary's cabin was located. Her hair was tied with a white satin ribbon, and in the dim moonlight she looked like some other-worldly angel who had happened to drop out of the sky onto Camp Little Wolf. There was a faint scent of lemon from her bubble bath.

She could hear the sound of crickets chattering in the trees and as she approached his door, a regular tapping issued from it. He was typing. She knocked lightly.

"Come in," he called, not turning around as he sat hunched over an ancient black Royal typewriter.

She felt awkward, wondering if it was too late to duck out. Just then he swung around in his chair to face her.

"Uh, you said if I needed to talk or something," Ferris began, smiling as her face grew warm despite the cool night air.

He looked surprised as he studied her standing uncertainly in the doorway. As he noticed her white gown, his expression reflected his attraction to her and also his caution. He smiled warmly, standing up.

"Here," he said, "let me get you something." He opened the door of a tiny refrigerator. "Coke?" he continued. "Milk? An apple?"

Ferris approached him, her nightgown flowing diaphanously. She pointed to a bottle of wine. "Some of that, please."

He shook his head. "You're under age."

"It'd help me talk—" she implored, reaching for the bottle.

"Nope." He took it from her, meeting her eyes sternly.

"But I drink wine at home all the time," she continued.

"No."

She shrugged, sending him a pouty look that he was treating her like a child. She studied the label of the wine bottle, saying snottily, "This isn't a very good year anyway."

He opened the refrigerator again. "How about some juice? I'll join you."

"Never mind," she retorted, sitting down on a makeshift couch covered with corduroy and several throw pillows. She arranged the folds of her nightgown as she posed, her head flung back, attempting to appear ethereal, romantic.

Gary grinned as he watched her, not unmoved by her loveliness. He cleared his throat, sitting down on a chair across from her. "So what's up, Ferris?"

She tossed her head so that her hair swung across her face, dropping her voice dramatically. "I envy Juliet . . ." She closed her eyes.

"Who?"

She smiled, placing her arms behind her neck. "You know, *Romeo and Juliet*. Didn't you read it? Everybody—"

"Oh," he said, perplexity crossing his face. "Juliet."

"Yes!" she cried. "Didn't you love it? So romantic yet so tragic, the star-crossed lovers . . ."

He stood up uncomfortably from his chair, crossing the room to open a window. "Hot night," he said. "You sure you don't want a Coke—or something?"

She opened her eyes, looking up at him, annoyed. "Oh . . ." she sighed. Then she got up and plunked herself down in his chair. "Oh . . ." she sighed once more.

He glanced at her suspiciously, aware that she wanted something but unsure exactly what it was.

"Dizzy . . ." she continued, spinning her head back and forth. When she dabbed at her forehead, he realized she was acting.

"You know, Ferris," he said shrewdly, "I don't think you're getting enough exercise."

She turned to him in disbelief. "What?"

"Tomorrow I'll ask Miss Nickels to take you on a thirty-mile hike . . ."

At first, she just gaped at him. Didn't he know? She was offering herself to him and he was talking about Miss Nickels and a thirty-mile hike. Maybe he wasn't getting her message somehow. So she crossed to where he sat on the couch and sat down very close to him.

He backed away a bit. She placed his hand on her cheek, moaning, "Oh, Gary. Can't you see? I'm burning up. I'm in the flower of my youth. At least Juliet died in her lover's arms . . . It would be worth it. She died . . ." Ferris paused theatrically. "Knowing—"

He bit his bottom lip to stifle the amusement that was beginning to rise in him. "Knowing what?" he asked.

She stared deeply into his eyes. "What it's like to be a woman." Her voice dropped to a whisper. "Oh, Gary, if only you knew . . ."

She gracefully floated off of the couch to the window, her nightgown billowing. "But it's too sad to talk about. And what's the use anyway?" She stared at the moon's quarter crescent. "Soon it'll all be over. *Tant pis . . .*"

"What are you talking about?" he demanded finally.

"I'm dying," she declared, touching her forehead. "The doctor said I only have"—she turned to him, her face tragic—"very little time left. Six weeks more of sweet life . . ."

Gary could no longer hold back his laughter and he let out a loud guffaw. Ferris covered her face, humiliated and hurt, and began to cry. He came over to her, saying softly, "C'mon, monkeyface. Hey, you . . ."

"No!" she cried. "Leave me alone!"

He put his arms around her. "What's happening, Ferris?"

"I have to become a woman," she sobbed.

"Oh," he said. "What's your definition of a woman?"

She looked at him. "An 'experienced' girl."

"You mean, sex?" he asked, smiling.

She blushed at the mention of the word, looking away from him. But then she nodded. "Yes," she said bravely.

He held her hand, but his voice was serious. "Making love won't turn you into a woman, Ferris. It doesn't work that way."

"I'm grown up enough!" she exclaimed. "Everybody's had all of those affairs and I haven't even been kissed for real." She continued to sob. "What's wrong with me? Why don't you want me?"

Gary pulled a Kleenex out of a box near his desk and handed it to Ferris. "Blow your nose."

"I'm not a child!" she protested, blowing her nose and then wiping her tears with her hand.

"I know that," he said.

"You're not worried about the difference in our ages, are you? In Europe it's acceptable for an older man to—uh, become involved with a younger girl. Haven't you read Colette's novels? Or Sagan? Remember, in *Bonjour Tristesse*—"

He listened patiently. "Ferris—"

"I don't understand," she continued. "We don't have to have a long affair. Just one night. We'll remember it forever."

Ferris reached for him and put her arms around his neck. As she kissed him, he started to respond. She could feel it.

"You sort of want me, don't you?" she whispered, pressing up closer to him. "Gary—"

He pulled away from her. "Maybe I do," he said. "But that's not really the point. To you, sex is . . ." He paused, searching for the right way to put it. Ferris winced once again at his calling it sex rather than love or romance. "Sex is poetry and phrases you've gotten out of books. Ferris, believe me, when you're really in love—"

"But I am, I really am. I've never felt this way

about anyone," she protested, clutching her heart to prove her sincerity.

"Maybe you think you are, but look at me. I'm not your prince . . . I'm a school teacher, no more, no less. Next year, you'll look at me and wonder how you could have thought you loved me."

"That's not true," she cried.

"Unfortunately it is." He studied her thoughtfully.

Ferris' expression became hopeful. "What if next year I come back and I still feel the same way? Would you—?"

He shook his head sadly.

She started crying again. "I'll be old then, Gary. Life will have passed me by. Do you know I'm almost the only virgin in camp? Everybody else knows this secret life—except me . . ."

"Poor thing," he teased, grinning.

"Look at it this way," Ferris suggested, giving it one final try. "It'd be a learning experience."

He chuckled and then opened the door.

"Where are you going?" Ferris asked.

"I'm walking you back."

She stared morosely at him. "Does it have to be that way? Bourgeois morality. Couldn't I just spend the night here? Just for appearance? We wouldn't have to do anything . . ."

He kept shaking his head back and forth patiently. "Let's go."

As they walked next to each other across the field to her cabin, Ferris implored, "What if I were twenty-one?"

He turned to her. "I'd probably fall madly in love with you."

"Honest?" she exclaimed, thrilled. "You really would?"

"Cross my heart," he said warmly.

"Oh!" Ferris squealed with excitement and delight, running away from him. Then she turned around and rushed back to Gary, kissing him clumsily on the lips.

25

RANDY recognized Angel's wolf whistle. He whistled back to answer her, grabbing his windbreaker as he ran out of the tent. The cool air shocked him awake.

"Where are you?" he whispered, shielding his eyes from the moon as he peered across the dark lake.

She whistled again.

"This is for the birds," he muttered as he took a canoe out and began paddling.

He whistled once more, looking around. She gave a tiny whistle in response. He could see her now. She was several feet ahead of him.

"How're you doing?" he asked, lighting a cigarette. Their boats were parallel, next to each other.

"Okay," she answered. "You want to get in?"

He climbed into Angel's rowboat, sitting down opposite her. He began, "I'm sorry about the other—"

"Stop apologizing," she interrupted.

"I'm sorry, I mean, oh, never mind. What's the matter?" he demanded, tying his boat to hers.

She continued rowing, not answering him. He

sighed loudly. "Women . . ." He shook his head in mock confusion.

As Angel rowed, she stared down at her sneakers, avoiding his eyes. He watched her intently, trying to figure her out. The night was silent except for the occasional caw of a bird flying by and the crickets in the trees. The water slapped steadily at the sides of the boat.

"Do you want to go to the boat house?" Randy asked finally.

Angel shrugged her shoulders, already rowing halfway in that direction. She was cold and scared. But it was too late to turn back. Besides, she assured herself, it wasn't such a big deal. Her eyes met his fleetingly, then dropped to the boat's bottom again.

When they got to the boat house, Randy leaped out of the boat and pulled it in. His canoe followed, banging behind it. He tied both of them to the log. Angel stood nearby, watching him. He walked over to her.

"You're shivering," he said tenderly, putting his arms around her.

She looked away, frightened. "Randy . . ." she began.

"Yeah?"

She bit her lip ferociously. "I feel kind of funny, uh, trembly . . ."

"You scared?" he asked.

She nodded. "A little . . ."

"Me too," he admitted.

Her expression revealed her surprise. "How come?"

"I don't know," he said, kicking a pebble near his shoe. "I thought a lot about you this week, you know."

"Me too," she confided shyly. "I mean, I like you,

I guess. When I first saw you, I thought you seemed nice."

He touched her hair. "Your hair's soft . . . It's funny," he said, smiling. "You talk rough and all, but your skin and hair—everything's soft."

"Is that okay?" she asked uncertainly.

"You kidding me?" he exclaimed. "It's fantastic!" He grinned broadly. "I can talk to you like a guy but—you're really—" He shook his head with admiration. "Are you still cold?" he asked.

She nodded.

"Let's go inside," he suggested.

"Okay," she said, following behind him.

When they were inside, he took her in his arms and kissed her. At first, she held back but soon she relaxed into his kiss, enjoying the feel of his mouth against hers.

"That was nice," she said, smiling.

"Yeah?" he asked, grinning proudly. "I've been around a little, you know?" He held her hand. "Some guys rush a girl," he continued, "but I don't."

"I appreciate it," she said sincerely. "Have you been here before?" Angel studied the wooden shack which she had once fled from. It looked different, somehow cozier.

"Sure. But not with a girl." He stared into her eyes. "I wouldn't bring you to a place I'd been to with somebody else. Why?" he asked, suddenly threatened. "You used the boat house before?"

She shook her head, saying, "It's quiet here."

"I come out here to think, you know," he said, laughing a little. "I don't look like anything's in my head, huh? But I have a lot going on in there."

"Have you thought about me—here?" Angel asked hopefully.

He nodded, embarrassed.

She grinned. "You don't have to say it," she whispered. "You know . . ." But her eyes held out for his sweet words, that it was something to him. That he liked her.

"I was really hoping we'd get together," he admitted. "I haven't been with anybody since I got to know you." He kissed her again.

Angel put her arms around his neck, holding on. "Randy, do you—don't laugh, please," she began. "But right this second, do you care about me a little?"

"A little," he mumbled, drawing her closer to him.

"I do too—a little . . ." she whispered, feeling all of the fears and resistance melt as they kissed.

26

FERRIS plopped down on her bed in an ecstatic heap. Her cheeks were red from the cool night air and her eyes glazed. She stared up at the ceiling dreamily.

Slowly Carrots, Sunshine and Cinder surrounded her in a curious circle. They studied her intently, looking at each other with excited anticipation. Chubby, Dana and Penelope joined them. Their expressions were dour and disappointed.

Soon Ferris' team began to cheer, jumping up and down, hugging each other. "Do you think so? I wouldn't be surprised—"

"It happened," Cinder pronounced triumphantly.

"Ferris did it?" Penelope asked. "How can you tell?"

"Look," Sunshine said. "Her face is all shiny."

"Yeah."

"She looks so happy."

"You're right."

"Yup," Dana said. Thinking that her team had lost, she tried to be a good sport. She grabbed Ferris' hand and attempted to shake it. "Congratulations," she said.

"Huh?" Ferris muttered absently.

Carrots raised Ferris' hand in the air. "The winner!"

Everyone started screaming and talking at the same time, running around the room in excitement. "We did it! We did it!"

Ferris looked up at them curiously. It had just dawned on her what was happening. As she was about to correct their assumption, she stopped herself. Carrots planted a kiss on her cheek. "Thanks, sport!" she cried.

"I knew Ferris would do it," Cinder said.

Everyone clustered around her bed, jabbering excitedly. Ferris smiled happily. They all accepted her. It was so easy. She almost believed it herself.

"He . . . he compared us to Romeo and Juliet," she recalled, sighing, staring at the moon out the window.

Sunshine moaned feverishly. "Oh, don't!"

Ferris continued, her voice passionate, "We drank some chilled Chablis and toasted each other that—"

"An aphrodisiac!" Dana gasped.

Carrots turned to Ferris. "Did it hurt at all?"

She shook her head. "It's the greatest experience I've ever had in my whole life!"

"You're such a child!" Cinder scolded Carrots.

"Did you see him naked?" Penelope inquired, her eyes wide with wonder.

"Don't be disgusting," Carrots chided Penelope.

Ferris looked shocked. "No, of course not." She turned to Cinder. "It was dark, you know."

"Then how'd he—?" Chubby asked suspiciously.

"The guy doesn't need a flashlight to do it," Cinder said impatiently.

"He didn't want to embarrass me," Ferris improvised. "So he shut off the lights. But the moon's silver light—"

"How cavalier," Dana commented.

"I'm going to die!" Sunshine gasped. "I really am. It's too much . . ."

Ferris closed her eyes as she spoke. "It was . . . perfect. The darkness enveloped us as he took me in his arms—"

"Oh, no!" Carrots squealed. "Then what happened?"

"Oh," Ferris sighed. "I guess nature took its course." She smiled beatifically. "He was strong but gentle, assured but also—I guess, a little bit shy." She looked at all of them. "So was I . . ."

"Did he say anything?" Penelope asked. "During it . . ."

Ferris continued, her face glowing. "Yes, I suppose he did. But words are meaningless then. It was how our bodies moved together."

"This is better than books!" Dana cried.

"The truth always is," Cinder replied wryly.

Ferris opened her eyes for a moment. "Yes, it is." Then she shut them again so that the romance on her movie screen could continue. The moon stared impenetrably through the window.

27

TEARS splattered from her eyes down her cheeks, dripping from her chin as she tried to button her shirt. Randy stood watching helplessly. He crouched down next to her. "Angel—"

"Don't look at me!" she cried.

He turned away, walking across the room to stare out the doorway. The night looked bleak to him. As he lit a cigarette, he wondered what he had done wrong.

Angel sat up slowly. She took a deep breath, wanting the tears to stop but they wouldn't, slobbering down all over her. What the hell was the matter with her?

"You can go if you want to," she said.

He turned to her, surprised and hurt. "Sure."

As he was about to step out the door, he looked back at her. She was struggling to put her jeans on, her body thin and frail. He sighed, not wanting to leave her. Didn't she like him anymore?

"Cigarette?" he asked, approaching her slowly.

She shook her head.

He hesitated, trying to think of something to say. "What'd I do wrong?" he blurted.

"Nothing."

"What's bugging you then?" he demanded.

"Nothing," she repeated. "I thought . . . it, uh, wasn't what I thought it'd be." She wiped her eyes with the back of her hand.

His expression revealed how crushed Randy felt. He had thought it was nice, that he had pleased her. "Oh," he said flatly, feeling inadequate.

"It was so personal," Angel said. "God, I felt really naked. Not my body. But like you could see into me, my head, what I was feeling . . ." She closed her eyes miserably, biting her lip. "I didn't know it'd be that way."

"I don't get you, man," Randy answered angrily. "One minute, you're—shit! Make up your mind! You came on to me—if you wanted to stop, you should of said something. No big deal." His voice grew rougher. "Plenty of women around . . ."

"I'm not a woman," she said softly, looking up at him. She wanted him to understand without having to tell him. "Making love's so . . . I don't know. It's just different from what I thought."

He was watching her, the realization suddenly hitting him in the back of the head. "You never did it before?" he asked, amazement in his voice.

She shook her head, staring down at the floor.

"Christ!" he exclaimed. "Why didn't you tell me?"

Angel shrugged, wiping her eyes again. He walked toward her. She said, "I thought it'd turn you off. You know, virgins are weird."

He scratched his head, impressed, awed. Then he gently touched her face. "You're something, you know that? You're beautiful!"

She felt confused, her feelings rising up and down

in her throat. "What are we supposed to do now?" she asked hopelessly.

He put his arm around her, wanting to protect her. "Angel, you're special . . ."

"I don't know anything," she muttered.

"I think I love you," he said, looking into her eyes. "I think I do!"

"You don't have to," she replied.

"I know."

He kissed her cheek, stroked her hair. Her voice dropped to a whisper as she spoke. "I feel so lonesome . . ." Angel started to weep again, unable to control her feelings. "What's happening to me!" she sobbed. "Christ almighty! I'm acting like Ferris. I don't cry. I never cry, not even when I was little and would skin my knee. I don't know what's wrong with me!"

She blew her nose ferociously, furious at her tears, for becoming so vulnerable, the tears spilling as if there were a leak somewhere inside of her. "If this is what sex is all about," she declared, "you can shove it! I'm not going to—"

"Angel—" Randy interrupted.

"What?" she demanded.

"Just hold on a minute, okay? Look, I told you I love you. I never said that to anybody before." He shook his head, smiling affectionately at her.

She stared at him, her face red, her eyes puffy, her nose runny, looking as if she'd sent her head through a washing machine cycle. Suddenly, she grinned. It was like the sun coming out after the flood, drying everything. He turned away uncomfortably.

"You're crazy," she said.

"So are you." He laughed with relief that she was

okay. "Angel . . ." he began, putting his arms around her.

"Don't," she said, almost in a whisper. "Please . . ."

"Are you afraid of me?" he asked, stepping back from her. He watched her tensely.

"No," she said, staring at the ground.

"Do you like me a little bit?" he asked gruffly, lighting a cigarette.

She nodded, wrapping her denim jacket tightly around herself.

"Then what?" he demanded.

Her eyes implored him. "Let's go, okay?"

28

SLOWLY and haltingly, Angel dragged herself back to the camp grounds. She was relieved to be alone at last. Maybe that way, in private, she would be able to sort out some of the thoughts and feelings that were rushing at her, confusing and tormenting her. Why was she so strung out? It was just sex. And there wasn't supposed to be anything to it.

She thought of the tender way that Randy had looked at her right before he had run back to his tent. His eyes were glowing and he smiled in a way that revealed affection but also something else. And they had kissed.

She had never seen so many stars in her whole life until she came up to camp. Some of them glowed so brightly, twinkling as if they were sending some sort of message. She could see the Big Dipper. Diane, her counselor, had pointed it out to her. Angel squinted and spotted the North Star. She traced the path of a shooting star with her finger.

It wasn't that she was turning into a nature freak, she knew that too. Angel walked so slowly she noticed

fire flies and even an old owl sitting on a branch—
anything to put off facing the girls in her cabin and
all their questions.

What would she tell them? She was never one to
lie and yet, this time, she wondered what to say. It
was almost better that she leave and never see any of
them again. She shook her head. That was dumb.
She'd have to tell them. It was part of the deal. But
the experience belonged to her alone—and Randy, of
course. She imagined the lines of his young body,
how strong it was, the smooth curves of his muscles.

They had started tentatively, their motions awkward. She hadn't known quite what to do, how to
do *it*. But he didn't rush her, gently caressing her.
She began to respond, her skin feeling awakened by
his touch. More and more, she wanted to open up
to him, give of herself. Soon she felt as if the bound-
aries between their bodies evaporated and she didn't
know who was touching whom, only that it was wonderful and right and fine.

It was only afterward that the rush of remorse
flooded her as he lay spent on top of her. She felt
trapped, pinned down by his body. She wanted desperately to split.

She peeked into the window of cabin A. Chubby
was asleep, a bag of Fritos on the floor next to her
bed. Carrots and Sunshine sat on the floor, playing
cards. Cinder was setting her hair, wearing her red
nightie. Dana sat near the door, watching it anxiously.

Angel took a deep breath. It was now or never.
She couldn't stand outside forever. Besides, she was
beginning to freeze her ass. She opened the screen
door quietly.

"It's Angel!" Dana screamed.

"If she did it, it's a tie!" Penelope shrieked.

Chubby bolted out of her bed. "Angel's here?" she inquired sleepily.

Carrots informed her as she entered, "Ferris and Gary did it."

"Angel," Dana said, peering at her. "Did you?"

"She looks different," Penelope commented hopefully.

"Please say yes. I bet my whole allowance on you . . ."

Angel studied them thoughtfully. She had still not decided what to say. She smiled unsurely.

"Well . . ." Cinder demanded, approaching her, her hair half set. She crossed her arms. "Ferris made it with Gary. What about you and Randy?" she demanded.

Finally, Angel shook her head. "I'm sorry," she told Dana, whose face dropped to her knees.

"Well," Dana said sorrowfully. "That's the breaks, I guess." She looked close to tears.

"Pay up," Cinder insisted, putting her hand out.

"Right now?" Dana asked.

She nodded coldly.

"Okay, already," Dana said, walking over to the night table next to her bed. She took out a red purse which she unzipped and removed several bills from it.

As the girls scurried about, collecting money and dividing it up on Cinder's bed, Ferris sat quietly, staring out the window. She did not want to face Angel.

Angel unlaced her sneakers and threw them on the floor. Then she got under the covers of her bed, with all her clothes on. Her expression was dazed. She lay there, her eyes wide open. Images of *it*, Randy, how he looked on top of her—darted through her mind.

Ferris turned to her hesitantly. "Hi," she said.

"Congratulations," Angel told her. "You won, fair and square." She tried to shake Ferris' hand.

Ferris held her hand back, shutting her eyes as guilt poured all over her like glue. She wanted to say something but knew she couldn't. Not then. She had lied but it hadn't felt like a lie.

"Angel," she began softly. "I'm sorry . . ." Her voice quavered.

Angel was already asleep, the cover clutched up to her chin.

Ferris sat down on her own bed, thinking of the girl who had been her adversary and then saved her life. In a funny way, she was relieved that Angel was still a virgin like herself.

She turned to look at the other girls who were making piles of the dollar bills.

"Okay, this is for cabin C," Cinder said officiously, sealing the bills in a Camp Little Wolf envelope. "We'll give it to them tomorrow at breakfast." She glanced at Dana. "Why don't you do it?"

"You really have to rub it in, don't you?" Dana remarked bitterly.

"I could have told you that Angel'd never do it," Cinder said. "Too scared. That whole tough act is a lot of bull."

Angel stirred momentarily, covering her face with the green camp blanket.

29

TALENT night was fast approaching. Dress rehearsal was called; cabin A, in full regalia of pastel-colored tutus and tights, practiced their modern dance skit. A girl with a long nose and black-frame glasses played the piano.

Randy sat down in a metal chair in the back row. He grinned as he watched Chubby leap through the air, her arms and legs outstretched. Sunshine followed from the wings, graceful and lithe, then Carrots, who slipped in the middle of the stage, bouncing hard on her behind.

"Ouch!" she screamed. "That didn't tickle."

Randy covered his mouth so that his loud howl would not be heard. The girls gathered around Carrots, chattering excitedly. "Time out!" Diane called. "Everybody take five minutes."

As Cinder walked past him, Randy remarked wryly, staring at her lime green tights, "Cute."

She smiled at him. "Looking for Angel?"

He nodded. "Could you do me a favor? Tell her, uh, I'll be at the boat house tonight. Okay?"

"Sure," Cinder said snottily. "But she won't come."

He grinned unsurely. "What are you talking about?"

"I just don't think she'll come," Cinder said, shrugging her shoulders. "But I'll tell her."

His expression revealed his confusion and hurt.

"She was using you," Cinder told him. "It was a game, dummy. Don't you see?"

"What do you mean?" Randy asked.

Cinder laughed merrily, seeing that he was getting upset. "We wanted to see who'd get laid first."

"I don't believe it," he muttered to himself. Then he turned to Cinder, trying to hide the fact that he was shocked and that her words were like a switchblade, cutting into him. "That chick's a real loser," he declared. "Hey, what're you doing tonight?"

She shot him a triumphant smile.

"I'll see you later," he said, still shaking his head with disbelief.

"EVERYBODY ON STAGE!" Diane called, cupping her hands.

"So long, baby," Cinder said. She held her tutu as she ran back to the stage.

Although he kept a grin on his face, Randy felt furious and crushed simultaneously. How could she have done that to him? And he had thought he loved her. What an idiot he had been.

Miss Nickels stormed into their cabin as the girls were putting on their CHAMP t-shirts. "Line up," she called.

Immediately, the girls dropped everything that they were doing, rushing to get into line and face Miss Nickels.

"What is this?" Carrots asked, under her breath.

"Dunno," Dana whispered.

"The girls in cabin A will not be represented in the Camp Little Wolf talent show," Miss Nickels announced.

"Aw!" Some of the girls groaned.

"That's not fair!"

"How come?"

"We went to all the rehearsals."

"Quiet!" Miss Nickels screamed, blowing her whistle. "Prophylactics were found in this cabin. In some volume, I might add. And certain girls stayed out past curfew . . ." Her eyes swept malevolently over Ferris and Angel, who stood next to each other in the line-up. "I've made my decision."

"That's not fair," Cinder complained.

"I haven't done anything," Dana added.

"How do you know it was us?"

"Yeah!"

"Do you have evidence?"

Miss Nickels blew her whistle again. "Girls!" she screeched. "We've never had such problems in this camp before. My mind is made up. You're all docked."

Sunshine burst into tears.

"Rumors are circulating that you girls are responsible for the taking of the Camp Little Wolf bus too. What do you have to say to that?"

"We would never do that," Carrots said.

"I can't even drive," Chubby added miserably.

"Even though all of you have denied it, the evidence points to you. What an unruly group . . ." She shook her head. "And many of you come from such good homes. What would your parents think?" She looked at Ferris, who dropped her eyes.

"What evidence is she talking about?" Carrots inquired.

"I feel sick," Sunshine moaned, grabbing her stomach.

Miss Nickels pulled out a foil-wrapped rubber from her pocket. "This was found in one of your drawers," she said like Sherlock Holmes. "And there were others in all of your drawers. I think your parents would be very interested to hear this."

"No!" Chubby screamed. "Don't tell them."

Dana shook her head sadly, peering at Miss Nickels' white tennis shoes.

"And last night," she began again, "I had a most disturbing call from one of our girls' parents . . ." She paused ominously. "The girl told her mother that someone in cabin A has been having an affair with a camp counselor."

All the girls turned to look at Ferris. Her face burned with shame.

"Girls, this is a very serious accusation," she continued. "If anyone knows anything about it, speak up immediately. We've already begun action against the counselor."

"Oh, no!" Ferris whispered.

"Such wickedness," she sneered. "What do you have to say?"

Cinder slowly raised her hand. She spoke hesitantly. "Well . . . Oh, God," she said. "I'll just die if he gets into trouble." She looked around, concern in her voice.

Ferris blanched visibly but she didn't speak.

Miss Nickels took a deep breath and said, her eyes scrutinizing each one of them, "Freedom is for those who can enjoy the privilege. Until camp ends, I'll be watching all of you. And you can forget about day trip, socials and especially the talent show. Do you have anything to say for yourselves?" she demanded.

The girls poked each other, nudging someone to say something. But everyone remained silent.

"All right, then," Miss Nickels concluded. "I've given instruction to the other counselors to be particularly vigilant with this group."

She slammed the screen door behind her.

30

***

ALL of Gary's belonging were piled on his bed. He dropped some shirts into an open plaid suitcase. Ferris watched from the doorway, pacing nervously. Finally she knocked softly. Her face was full of anxiety.

He turned around, startled from his thoughts. When he saw Ferris, he smiled sarcastically. "Well, if it isn't Mata Hari . . ."

"Could we talk? Please?" she urged him.

"Why not?" he said. "We're lovers, aren't we?" His arms were crossed, his eyes burned with anger.

Ferris walked into the room slowly, looking at the walls that were stripped of his books. "Did they really fire you?" she asked, astonished.

"Well, what the hell did you think?" he demanded. "According to Miss Nickels, I'm a 'sexual deviant.'" He stared at her, shaking his head ruefully. "Why?" he asked. "Why'd you—I thought you were a nice kid. Sensitive, intelligent. You're a goddamn fraud. And I fell for it. That's what you are." He turned from her. "I've got a lot of packing to do, so you better—"

"I'm not!" Ferris cried. "I'm really not that way."

He darted around to face her. She backed off, afraid of his anger. "You owe me an explanation, don't you think?" he said.

"I'm sorry," she whispered.

"That's not good enough." He grabbed her by the arm. "Talk to me, damn it. Why'd you do it? I still don't understand."

She searched the walls for something to fasten her eyes onto, to avoid his. She found a calendar, focusing on the bold black numbers.

"What is it?" he interrogated. "You get your kicks this way or something?" He dropped her arm. "Screwing around with other people's lives?"

She closed her eyes, taking a deep breath. Then she said in almost a whisper, "I wanted the girls to like me . . ." At the sound of her own words, she broke down and began to sob. Ferris covered her face with her arm miserably.

He watched her, his eyes narrowed suspiciously. But soon, a half-grin formed on his face as he recognized the truth in her answer. "Say that again," he declared.

"I wanted to be in," she confessed. "Just once." Sobs wrenched her body. "I didn't want to be the rich kid that everybody hated."

"So you made up that story about—"

"No!" she interrupted. "Well, yes. Not exactly. You see, I tried to tell the truth. I really did."

"You didn't try hard enough."

"Nobody would listen to me. Please, Mr. Callahan—"

"Call me Gary," he said. "After all, we've been intimate, right?"

"We have been, sort of!" Ferris blurted. "I wanted—"

He scrutinized her, scratching his head with amazement.

"I mean," she amended herself, "I wish we could have been . . ." Her voice trailed off, lost in her sobs. "I almost believed it."

He sighed, no longer angry at her, understanding, even feeling a little bit sorry for Ferris. He turned to stare bitterly at his bed where all his possessions awaited his packing. "That's why you started this—"

"Yes," she admitted. "I told them stuff that, uh, I guess, I wanted to be. So much—" She smiled slightly as the tears fell all over her t-shirt.

"But you must have known—" he began.

"It didn't feel like a lie!" she exclaimed. "Sometimes I thought it might actually happen. You even said so yourself, if I was older—remember?" Her voice implored him.

She tried to make them stop, the tears that were streaming down her cheeks but to no avail. "I didn't mean to get you into trouble," she wailed. "I'm so ashamed."

He approached her, putting his arms around her. "Hey, I know that." Gary grabbed a shirt from his suitcase and wiped the tears from her face. "Just don't blow your nose—"

"You'll hate me forever," she said. "And I don't blame you." She covered her eyes with her hands.

"Nah," he replied. "If I was your age, I might have done the same thing." He shrugged his shoulders. "Really."

"Not you," Ferris interrupted. "No, you're—oh, I don't know!" She hugged him, crying desperately.

"Come on, you," he said affectionately. "Everything'll be okay . . ." They both stared at his suitcase.

"But you've lost your job," she declared. "What are you going to do?"

"I really don't know," he confided. "I'll do something." He looked hopelessly around. How had he become entangled in this adolescent mess?

"I guess it's too late to say I'm sorry," Ferris dropped her voice. "But I really am."

"I know that."

"Suppose I told them?" she suggested.

"Who?"

"Miss Nickels. Maybe then, I don't know, it might change things . . ."

He shook his head. "Forget it. As you said, it's too late." His eyes met hers momentarily. "Maybe you learned something . . ."

"I did!" Ferris exclaimed. "I love you, Mr. Callahan," she declared, running out of the room.

31

CABIN A had to sit in the Camp Little Wolf out-door theater, watching glumly as all the other cabins performed renditions of the *Rocky Horror Picture Show* and other skits for Talent Night. Angel walked in after it had begun, taking a seat in the back row.

She knew that the boys from Camp Tomahawk were invited and she searched for Randy, who had not met her at the appointed time at the boat house. All of a sudden, she spotted him. She felt a chill travel from the top to the bottom of her spine. He was sitting next to Cinder, whose hair was plaited in a multitude of braids, each braidlet ending in a silver bead. When he saw Angel, he deliberately put his arm around Cinder. Angel glared angrily. Cinder giggled, whispering something in Randy's ear.

Angel tried to ignore them, fixing her attention on three girls from cabin C who were singing their own version of the Bee Gees' *Stayin' Alive*. One of the girls, a gangly redhead with thick glasses, played electric guitar. The sound was enough to drive the birds in the trees south several months before their scheduled time.

When he thought she wouldn't see him, Randy

sneaked a glance in the back to see Angel. She stared down at the ground. When she looked up and met his eyes, he turned around immediately, squeezing Cinder's shoulder. Angel sucked her teeth, muttering to herself, "The bastard, the creep. Shit!" But she didn't want to give him the satisfaction that he was actually getting to her—which he was, in spades. Damn him!

She just couldn't understand it. What the hell was wrong with him? The last time they saw each other, he said he would meet her at the boat house. Even though she hadn't heard from him, she went to their meeting place. But no one was there.

He had said he loved her, hadn't he?

Finally, when she couldn't stand another moment of it, she started to walk away. She didn't know where she would go, but she had to get out of this place. Her mother was right. Men were creeps. Every one of them.

Soon she began to run, trying to run away from her own feelings which followed her like a shadow. She didn't want to break down, not with him there and that bitch, Cinder. When she slowed down, she heard her name called.

"Angel! Hey, wait up!" Randy screamed.

She started running again, faster and faster. What did he want? She ran past the cabins to the outskirts of the camp grounds.

"I want to talk to you!" he called.

She slowed down, allowing him to catch up with her. They stood facing each other, anger and hurt in both of their faces. "What do you want?" she demanded. "Long time no see. How's Cinder?"

"How much did you make?" he asked, brushing his hair out of his face with his hand.

She looked puzzled. "What do you mean?"

"Don't bull me. I know all about it. The contest . . ." he said contemptuously. "How much did you make off of it?"

She moved away from him, her cheeks beginning to burn.

"Why didn't you tell me it was a game?" he demanded, shrugging his shoulders. "I would of gone along with it." He studied her. "An easy lay is an easy lay . . ."

Angel's expression revealed her dismay at his words. "I lost," she said quietly.

He studied her suspiciously.

"I didn't win, creep," she admitted. "Get it? I didn't tell them, for your information."

"You mean, you let yourself lose?" he asked.

She looked down unhappily. "I'm a loser. I always lose, no matter what I do."

He moved closer to her, dropping his voice gently. "No, you're not."

"Oh, yeah?" she said. "We could have been friends, hung out together and had some good times."

"You're something else!" he exclaimed. "I should have trusted you . . . Angel, let's give it another chance. Okay? We could——"

"We can't just hold hands," she interrupted. "It's too late. We started in the middle. We never even had a beginning." Her eyes were dark with regret.

"It doesn't have to be that way," Randy argued. "We could try. If you gave me your phone number, I could call and we could go to the movies or whatever——"

She shook her head. "It would be weird."

"We wouldn't even have to see each other," he said. "If you don't want. We'll just talk—or write letters, I don't know!" He glanced anxiously at her.

"Let's walk," Angel suggested, feeling there was

safety in movement. She didn't want to stand there and start bawling like a sobsister.

As they walked next to each other, Randy took her hand. "Why not?" he asked her. "Why can't we see each other?"

"Because it wouldn't be enough—for either of us!" She blurted the words out. "I can't handle it."

"Angel—" He took her in his arms. "I care about you. I really do."

"Don't," she implored him, pushing him away.

"Why?" he asked. "Don't you like me?"

She kissed him, brushing his lips quickly. "I'll never forget you. I swear!"

As she walked away from him, Randy began to follow her but he stopped himself. If she came back of her own will, he'd be there, waiting.

Angel turned around for a moment, waving. "See you around, sucker!" she called. But her heart felt suspended by a thin blue thread.

32

Her head was swimming, back and forth, all over the place with no destination. She wandered around the camp grounds, picking up pebbles and pitching them, trying to calm down, to make some sense of all the crap which was confusing her and making her feel unsure. How had it all turned into such a mess? She wanted to understand.

As Angel approached the empty play area where the tykes usually see-sawed and climbed the monkey bars, she spotted Ferris sitting on a swing, swaying back and forth listlessly.

At first, she wanted to head back in the opposite direction. Solitude was what she needed, not girl chit-chat. But when Ferris looked up, she smiled wryly at her. Angel shrugged her shoulders and jogged over to the swings.

She grabbed the adjacent swing, pumping lightly with her legs. Ferris took off too, raising her legs at an acute angle. Soon both of their swings arched past the top of the treelines, then dipped down and rose on the other side.

Ferris giggled nervously, allowing her legs to

dangle so that the swing would slow down. Angel did the same thing. Now they sat next to each other, tanned legs outstretched, watching some birds fly by.

"How's Randy?" Ferris asked.

Angel looked at her, about to dissemble and bullshit, but she figured why should she bother. "We just broke up," she answered grimly.

"Oh." Ferris glanced at her sympathetically. Angel, whose face was set, her jaw jutting out, could not hide her anguish. She stared down at the ground glumly.

Ferris wanted to ask her more but she held back. She had already learned how much Angel valued her privacy. She swayed on the swing, forming a small arc.

Angel turned to her abruptly. "Hey, do you feel any different?" she asked.

"What do you mean?"

"You know. Since you did it . . ."

"Uh," Ferris gulped, shame crossing her face. But she couldn't admit the truth, not yet. "Well, no," she said, wishing she could tell her. "Not really."

"I mean," Angel said, searching for the right way to express herself, "was it what you thought it would be?" She bit her bottom lip with embarrassment, reaching out to Ferris to confirm her own experience.

Ferris tried to change the subject, afraid of being caught in her own ignorance. "No big deal," she said.

Angel's expression grew more confused. "Everybody says that but . . ." she began, then changed her mind. "Well, now you're a woman," she said, smiling wryly.

Suddenly Ferris' words tore out of her fiercely. "Bull!" she cried. "My whole affair was a lie. He didn't even touch me!"

"You're kidding!" Angel laughed aloud, aware of the irony. Everything had turned out so ridiculous.

"What's so funny?" Ferris demanded.

"Nothing," she answered, shaking her head. "You want to know something? Oh, never mind . . ."

"No, tell me," Ferris urged her.

"Okay, but I'll kill you if you tell anybody. Me and Randy, uh, you know . . ." She was unable to say it but Ferris understood. "We . . ."

"Gosh," Ferris said, her eyes wide with amazement.

Angel nodded ruefully. Both girls sighed loudly, weighed down by their experiences and, in Ferris' case, her lack of it and the ensuing lie.

"Gosh," she repeated, feeling sorry for Angel, overwhelmed by it all.

"Is that all you can say?" Angel asked, trying to act tough. "For somebody who's been all over, you have a lousy vocabulary."

"It's just that," Ferris began. "You know, we've both been such fools."

"I know."

"First-class morons," Ferris added.

"Assholes."

"Dupes—"

"Suckers," Angel interrupted.

"Asinine, intimidated . . ."

"Speak for yourself," Angel said, cracking up.

For a moment, Ferris was about to react as if she were insulted but instead she began laughing with Angel. "You're right," she admitted. "I am."

"So am I."

33

AFTER breakfast they all piled out of the mess hall. Carrots said, "My mom will disown me. She really will."

"Couldn't we just write an anonymous note or something?" Dana asked, poking Sunshine in the ribs with her finger.

"Hey, quit it!" she complained. "My parents told me never to gamble. If they find out, they'll definitely make me go into est."

Angel and Ferris stood together, surrounded by the other girls. Everyone was talking at once.

"We're telling Nickels," Angel declared, walking ahead of them. "If you don't like it, shove it. We're all in this."

Cinder stamped her foot. "For God's sake, what good will telling her do?"

"We'll get Gary out of trouble, if we're lucky," Ferris added, glaring at her.

"You're all so naive," Cinder said. "I can't believe it. We'll end up looking ridiculous. That's all."

"I don't give a shit," Angel muttered, continuing to walk. The other girls hastened their pace to catch up with her. "She looks like she really means it," Chubby whispered.

"Hey, wait up!" Carrots called.

"We only have two more days of camp," Cinder said. "Why blow it?"

"I say we should have a vote on this," Dana suggested.

Penelope ran up and stood on the flagpole mound. "I vote we take the secret to our graves."

Chubby nodded. "I second it."

Angel turned to them angrily. "There's nothing to vote about. What are you all so afraid of?"

Cinder's eyes narrowed. "Nickels won't believe her anyway," she said conspiratorially. "She'll just think she's trying to protect her lover." Her voice dropped. "Especially if we all stick together . . ."

Carrots looked uncomfortably around herself. "I, uh, think Angel and Ferris may be right."

Cinder rolled her eyes. "Aren't we bourgeois?" she remarked sarcastically.

Ferris whispered to Angel, covering her mouth with a cupped hand. "What if they all deny it?"

Angel shrugged her shoulders. "That's life."

Carrots, who had been caught offguard by Cinder's remark, said slowly, "Maybe I am bourgeois. I can't help it."

Cinder crossed her arms. "If you two talk, we'll never speak to you again. Ever!"

Ferris looked at her. "I really don't care. So shove it." She walked away from her. Angel nodded.

Cinder gathered the other girls around her. "We'll deny it all. They'll never believe her. If we stick together, it'll look like Angel and Ferris are—"

"Shut your face," Angel sneered.

"Don't talk to me like that!"

"I'll talk to you any way I please!"

Chubby stood up to Cinder, her arms crossed. "You think you're so special 'cause you're a model. I'd rather be fat and feel good inside!"

"Wow," Angel muttered under her breath.

"Who cares what you think?" Cinder said, raising her voice.

"I do," Dana said. "She's my friend."

Cinder groaned. "I don't believe any of you." She stared contemptuously at all of them.

"I vote yes!" Sunshine said. "We tell Nickels."

"Me too," Dana said. "Just so long as Angel and Ferris do the talking."

"I'd die!" Carrots confided.

"Idiots!" Cinder yelled, her voice growing shrill.

Sunshine put her arm around Ferris' shoulders. "You know, I'm glad you and Gary didn't—uh, fool around. Kissing's more romantic."

Angel heard her and smiled ruefully.

"What do you know?" Cinder demanded.

"Nothing." Sunshine met her eyes icily.

"Ah," Cinder said. "A third virgin. How quaint."

Dana walked up behind her, saying, "Uh, make that four, will you?"

"Me too!" Carrots added. "What do you know!"

They all shook hands, giving each other "five" in agreement.

By this time, Cinder was livid. "You're absolutely cherubic," she cried with disgust. "How cute."

Sunshine turned to her, her usually peaceful countenance transformed. She stepped back and socked Cinder in the face.

"How dare you!" Cinder screamed. She patted her face to make sure there was no damage. "Don't ever hit my face!" she howled. "Ever! Do you hear me!"

"You . . . fraud," Sunshine said, joining the others.

"C'mon," Angel called. "Let's go," she told Ferris. They walked toward Miss Nickels' office together.

"Wait for us!" Dana cried. "We're coming too."

Chubby followed with her after them. "As long as we don't have to say anything," she said.

Carrots walked over to Sunshine. "You've got a pretty good right," she said. "I wouldn't have ever thought it, you're so . . . How'd you do it?"

Sunshine made a muscle with her arm. "B-12."

They laughed together, following the others. Only Cinder stayed behind, stamping her foot angrily, screeching, "You bitches! You stupid little bitches! You can drop dead for all I care. You'll never make it anywhere! You're just losers! Losers! Do you hear me!"

34

CABIN A looked like catastrophe had hit. Actually it was just the girls packing their belongings to go home.

Underwear, sweat socks, t-shirts flew around the large room. "Hey, those are mine!" Chubby called, pointing to an oversize pair of running shorts.

Penelope held them up in the air. "You're right," she said. "Here!" She threw them across to her.

Dana resembled an auctioneer as she called, "And how much am I offered for a stack of sexy books?" She held them up in the air.

"I'll give you my whole allowance for the summer," Penelope answered. "But it's only five dollars."

"Forget it," Dana said firmly. "Anybody else want to place a bid?"

"Can I really keep your sweater?" Carrots asked Sunshine as she wrapped the beautiful wheat-colored sweater around her.

"Sure," she said. "I've been searching for a pair of jeans that fit like these."

They hugged each other excitedly.

Penelope implored, "I could send you some more money once I get home . . ."

Dana smiled. "Oh, okay. But I'm warning you. You're going to be tested on the material."

Penelope ran up and took the pile from her. "Gee, thanks a lot!" When she pulled out the five-dollar bill from a small leather disco bag, Dana shook her head. "Save it for another training bra."

Cinder's wardrobe was neatly set out in piles on her bed. She packed without saying a word to any of them. As she turned around to take down one of the photographs of herself hanging over her bed her enormous black eye was revealed.

Carrots pointed to her while her back was turned. "Whoa! You really did it!" she whispered.

Sunshine nodded. "I couldn't help it."

Penelope packed the books into her suitcase, saying, "You know, I once saw some people doing it on the beach."

"Yuck!" Chubby muttered.

Penelope added, "It wasn't at all like in the movies . . ."

"What happened?" Carrots asked, her interest fanned.

"I walked in on my parents once," Chubby declared.

"That's totally gross!" Carrots exclaimed.

"Parents are too old to do it," Dana said. "I think the last time mine did it was when I was conceived. And they've regretted it since." She grinned.

"The man had sand all over his back," Penelope continued. "It wasn't romantic at all."

"I'm never giving in," Chubby said, crossing her arms. "Unless I have to, at gunpoint or something."

"Me neither."

"I'd rather talk about it than do it."

Ferris waited for Angel before getting on the bus. As Angel climbed the stairs, carrying her torn plaid suitcase, Ferris followed with her designer luggage.

"You're breathing down my neck," Angel complained. "For God's sakes!"

Ferris plunked down in the seat next to Angel, who felt like smiling but instead frowned. She was undaunted. "Won't it be great to get out of this prison?" Ferris said.

Angel didn't answer, shrugging her shoulders indifferently. But as the yellow run-down Camp Little Wolf bus took off, she thought of their heist and shook her head with amusement.

Ferris stared out the window. It hadn't been a bad summer, after all. And she had made a new friend. Or had she? She turned to look at Angel. For a moment, their eyes met. Then Angel said, "I warned you about this . . ."

"Oh, right," Ferris said, pretending to be intimidated by Angel's toughness. But she wasn't anymore. She had seen through it to the soft, vulnerable side of her friend.

The bus was noisy. Some of the girls sang "One hundred bottles of beer on the wall . . ." while others told dirty jokes and disseminated sexual misinformation.

"So if you do that before, you can't get pregnant."

"Are you sure?"

"Just take a really hot bath. Spermatazoa can't live because it's too hot in there."

"I just don't know. I never heard of it."

Cinder sat apart, wearing a sophisticated dark dress. Her injured eye was covered by dark glasses.

As Ferris studied her, she thought how much older Cinder looked than the others.

Angel interrupted her thoughts. "Hear from your mother?" she asked.

"She doesn't want to be married anymore," Ferris said nonchalantly, but there was anger in her voice. "She's going to open a boutique in Manhattan. She wants to find herself."

Angel's expression revealed her surprise. "Isn't that something," she said.

"Yeah."

A silence followed for several minutes in which each of them wanted to say something to the other. Finally Ferris broke it. "Guess I won't be seeing you again, huh?" she said softly.

"Big deal," Angel said.

"Never mind," she replied, looking back out the window. Suddenly Ferris felt waves of depression heading her way. What did she have to look forward to? Her father and her together, with nothing to say to each other. It would be hell. She knew it.

Angel's arms were folded tightly around her chest. She too thought about what awaited her. Somehow it gave her comfort to be sitting with Ferris. But she didn't want to admit it to herself.

Carrots leaned over their seat. "How's it going, guys?"

They both grinned, Angel pulling one of her long red braids. "You should be more careful, Rapunzel," she said.

As the bus pulled into the Sportsorama parking lot and some of the girls spotted their parents, a loud groan circulated through the bus.

"I don't want to go home, I don't want to go home," several girls who stood on their seats sang. "I want to stay at camp where I can be a tramp.

Oh, dear, what can the matter be? I don't want to go home . . ." After they finished, everyone applauded riotously.

Ferris saw her father's Rolls immediately. He stood leaning against it, looking tired. Her heart did a somersault. She waved anxiously. He couldn't see her yet.

Angel also spotted their old Chevy. Her mother sat in the driver's seat, smoking a cigarette. Angel reached for her own pack and discovered it was empty. "Darn," she grumbled.

Both of them stood on tiptoe, reaching for their suitcases. Ferris was the first one out. As she climbed down the stairs, she saw Gary walking over to the bus.

"Oh, no," she whispered. Ferris had not seen him since that last time. She wasn't even sure she would ever see him again. And now he was there, walking over to her. She didn't know what to do.

As she tried to duck past him, he reached out and grabbed her hand. She shifted her weight from foot to foot awkwardly, aware that the other girls were watching them.

"You're quite a woman, Miss Whitney," he said.

She looked up at him. He rumpled her hair affectionately. Ferris broke into an enormous grin. "Wait'll I'm twenty-one," she warned him. "Just you wait, Mr. Callahan."

35

FERRIS had difficulty meeting her father's eyes as she approached him. He had lost some weight and he looked disheveled. The divorce was showing. But he smiled bravely.

"Oh, Dad!" she cried as they embraced. He was reluctant to let go. "I can't breathe," she said finally.

"How are you?" he asked.

She nodded, smiling. "Okay. And you?"

"I'm getting used to it. What can I say? But you look terrific. So tan . . ."

Ferris turned around, following Angel with her eyes. She was dragging her mother across the parking lot.

"I want to talk to you," Angel demanded.

"Yeah?" Her mother wore a low-cut flowered dress that was short and tight. She hobbled in her high heels. "Hey, slow down. What's the rush?" she asked. "So what do you want to talk about?"

"Sex," Angel said. "You better straighten up your act, Mom. What's this crap about it being nothing?"

She was clearly taken aback by her daughter's remark. She managed a soft, "Oh."

"You been hanging around with creeps and that's going to change," Angel continued.

"Now you wait a minute," her mother said, squinting at her daughter.

"No!" she exclaimed. "I'm keeping my eye on you from now on. What are you?" Angel asked. "Forty years old?"

"Are you kidding! I'm twenty-nine," she said, smiling coyly at the transparency of her own lie.

"And you still don't know the facts of life," Angel declared. "Jeez!"

From her boyfriend's Land Rover, Cinder watched the other girls. As they embraced, she adjusted her sunglasses.

"How are you, baby?" her boyfriend whispered.

"Not bad," she said.

"Did you miss me?"

"You know I did," Cinder muttered, but it was the other girls who were the focus of her attention. "I thought about you all the time."

Sunshine leaned out of her family's Day-Glo van. "Remember to take your vitamins!" she called to Carrots and Dana. "Especially the Bs. See you next July!"

Penelope, who dragged her suitcase on the ground since it was loaded with Dana's books, was met by an elderly, grandmotherly woman who offered to help her carry them.

"Oh, no!" Penelope cried. "I can do it."

"Did you learn a lot of new things this summer?" she asked innocently.

"Oh, yes," Penelope said. "You wouldn't believe all the things I learned."

"Did you take nature walks?"

"Sure. Birds. Bees. And lots of trees."

As Ferris began to climb into the Rolls, she heard a tough voice call, "Wait a minute, sucker!"

Her face beamed as she looked up to discover Angel dragging her mother, who was trying to pull down the skirt of her dress as she walked.

"This is my—" Angel began, pausing momentarily. "What the hell—my friend, Ferris Whitney." She stopped herself, then added, "My best friend . . ."

Ferris got out of the car and threw her arms around Angel happily. "How's it going!"

Angel grinned at her mother and Ferris' father. "She can be such an ass sometimes. Don't mind her . . ."

"Screw you!" Ferris cried, laughing.

"Heavens!" Angel exclaimed. "Look at the kind of language she's learned."

Ferris' father looked helplessly at the girls, wondering whether to be concerned about the possible influence on his daughter or relieved that she had found a friend.

Ferris climbed back into the car when he started the motor. She yelled out of the window to Angel who was already in her mother's jalopy. Both motors were revving.

"Hey, creep! I'm listed in the phone book."

"Me too!" Angel cried over the volume of the Chevy's coughing motor.

The cars pulled away parallel to each other. The girls continued to call excitedly to each other, alternating insults with affectionate taunts.

"What is that?" Angel hooted. "A hearse?"

Ferris laughed. "Yours looks like an accordion!"

"Where's the funeral?"

"Where's the junkyard?"

As the cars approached the parking lot exit, Angel screamed, "Call me tomorrow!"

Ferris feigned surprise. "*You* have a phone?"

"Ferris," her father said. "That's not a very nice thing to say."

"No, dummy!" Angel yelled, leaning out the window. "Just call from the street!"

As their cars began to turn in opposite directions, Ferris shouted, "I'll call you first thing in the morning!"

Angel waved until the Rolls disappeared around the corner. Then she slumped into the seat next to her mother who watched her daughter curiously.

"Don't say a word—"

"I wasn't—"

"Okay."

A contented smile flashed across Angel's face.